The Tenancy

The Tenancy

Eva Figes

SINCLAIR-STEVENSON

First published in Great Britain 1993
by Sinclair-Stevenson Ltd
an imprint of Reed Consumer Books Ltd
Michelin House, 81 Fulham Road, London SW3 6RB
and Auckland, Melbourne, Singapore and Toronto

A CIP catalogue record for this book
is available at the British Library

ISBN 1 85619 305 5

Typeset by Deltatype Ltd, Ellesmere Port
Printed in Great Britain by Butler & Tanner Ltd, Frome

. I .

They came to take Edith's mother away on a particularly fine spring morning in early May. Edith was struck by this odd contrast as she waited for them to come to the house, strongly suggesting, as it did, cold indifference at the heart of the universe. Dazzling sunlight glorified everything, old walls, old trees, rooftops, and she had been hearing birdsong since before dawn. She saw the two men walking up the front path in their shirtsleeves, under the falling laburnum.

Edith had everything ready. She held open her own front door, on the second floor, and listened to them talking as they came up the stairs. They continued to talk, to her now, and then to Mrs Johnson as they lifted her into a chair and wrapped a bright red blanket round her. They were used to this sort of thing, and had a special chair to manoeuvre people down from upper floors. But Mrs Johnson did not respond. She kept her eyes closed, and her eyelids did not so much as flicker as they lifted her cautiously down the staircase, floor by floor, then down the front steps to the open doors of the ambulance. Edith, following behind, felt, rather angrily, that this was one more sign of her mother's stubborn dislike of the house, which she had made all too clear from the day she moved in.

This was still her overriding emotion after she had watched the white vehicle drive off and turned, at last, to the building which had once, but not for many years, been her own home. Edith stood for a moment under the hanging laburnum, smelling the spring sunshine, before slowly climbing the stairs to her flat. Though at long last she was by herself once more, she knew this would take some getting used to. There was not just a lot of tidying up to do. It was necessary to go over old ground in order to go forward. So much clutter, and not only in her rooms.

She knew it was unkind of her to resent her mother's expression as the men carried her out. She was old, and ill. But the shut eyes, the down-turned mouth, her very silence told Edith what she had been hearing for far too long.

Beggars cannot be choosers, she would sigh, and not merely during those first days and weeks when she had to adjust to moving in, having nowhere else to go. She never got used to it, or rather, simply got used to grumbling. She continued to complain about the two flights of stairs, the lack of effective heating, the draughty sash windows, and spoke of ending her days as a burden on her daughter. From her tone it was obvious that she considered the burden to be hers rather than Edith's.

Edith was hurt by all this. She tried to shrug off the unending sniping and whining as a characteristic of old

2

age. When the two of them were alone she usually pretended not to have heard; in the presence of a visitor she shrugged and smiled with apologetic irony behind the old girl's back. Nevertheless, it was wounding.

Mrs Johnson liked, in the presence of a visitor, to make it clearly understood that she had come down in the world. She was not used, she said, to living in a flat, and in an old house which should, in her opinion, have been pulled down long ago. In earlier, happier times she had possessed her own little house, very modern and labour-saving. She would fondly recall the minor features of this house, which was newly built when she, newly married, had moved in. She was proud of the fact that nobody had lived in the house before her, and if she had been told then that she would end up in such a ramshackle old house, in a converted flat, it would have broken her heart. But then, winding up with a heavy sigh, beggars cannot be choosers.

It went round and round in her head now, this summing up, the unending sound of her mother's voice, as she shut her front door on silence for the first time in years. It had also been embarrassing, since the visitor who had to listen to old Mrs Johnson was either a tenant in the same house, or a similar building in the neighbourhood. Edith did not have many visitors, and the number dwindled after she began caring for her mother.

It was water dripping on stone, thought Edith, suddenly lost in the silence, the empty rooms, vacated space. Except that the relentless dripping had not been on anything so hard, it had worn a pit in her unprotected innards, where her mother's child was hiding, even now, after so many years.

Edith stood at a window, gazing out at the brightness,

but saw nothing. Of course, she thought, her fury beginning to simmer, the reason for her so-called beggary was never mentioned, not ever. In all the years Mrs Johnson had not once so much as hinted that something had occurred, that her decline in status, this lamentable dependency on her daughter, was anything other than an act of God, or simply the result of tragic widowhood. Edith could have understood and forgiven if Mrs Johnson had been trying to avoid washing dirty linen in public, but she spoke and acted in precisely the same way when she and Edith were on their own. It was as though the entire incident had been blotted out from her mind, and with it her own gullible stupidity and darling Robert's criminal misconduct. Instead she nurtured only a vague sense of grievance, against the world in general and, this being too indistinct a target, against Edith in particular.

Darling Robert. It was always when she thought of her brother and his part in all this that her resentment reached boiling point, and it did now. She told herself that she would have to tell him about mother, but not now. Much he cared, they had not heard from him in weeks. Besides, he would be out of the house and she was in no mood to speak to that awful wife of his. Edith lifted the heavy sash so the mild spring air could blow in. Below her a child was skipping along the pavement, wearing a school blazer and a leather satchel which flapped at her back. Edith saw that her hair was tied up in bunches before the small figure vanished under the blossoming laburnum. She felt a sharp stab of anguish at this sight. How fleeting it all was, the carefree jumping and running under a morning sky, blue, without a cloud in it. For me, she thought, it had begun to grow dark and cloudy when I was not much bigger than

4

that child. I had scarcely begun to sprout breasts or body hair when my mother began nagging at me, constantly finding fault, I could not do a thing right. I had the wrong body, or the spirit in it was wayward. It kept doing and saying things it should not do or say. It was as though the house in which Edith had been living for so many years, ever since she left home, was but an extension, an outward and visible sign of what was wrong, had always been wrong, with Edith. And so her mother continued to carp at the unsatisfactory surroundings she was now obliged to share with her unmarried daughter.

Edith turned away from the window, thinking she must begin to tidy up, but she drifted aimlessly, standing, touching things, moving purposively to the door, only to forget why she had done so. She was still immersed in the past, drowning in it. Her unmarried daughter: that was it, in a nutshell. Mrs Johnson was nothing if not outspoken, and she made no secret of the fact, to almost anyone willing to listen, that she thought Edith had made a mess of her life. Even as a child she would not do as she was told, and as for making the most of herself, well, you see the result. She could have found a husband, if she had not been so choosy, if she had done something about her hair, if she had not been so wilful, always thinking about herself, putting herself first, refusing to wear a girdle. Mrs Johnson had bought Edith a girdle on her fourteenth birthday. On her fifteenth birthday she took her to the local hairdresser for permanent waving, so her hair was brittle and frizzy before it grew out. At about the same time her mother decided it was time her daughter knew how to cook, and she was required to help cook Sunday lunch each week, always a roast of some sort with two vegetables. By the time she was sixteen she knew how to prepare mashed potatoes, roast potatoes, thicken gravy, and boil the most common sorts of greens.

Mrs Johnson felt she had done her best for her daughter. I warned you, didn't I always warn you? God knows I did my best, but it was like talking to the wall. Edith could still hear the familiar litany, echoing down the long years. She had let her mother down, no doubt about that. As far as Mrs Johnson was concerned, Edith was a failure. She found herself standing in front of the bathroom mirror, not knowing why, staring accusingly into the fading eyes of an oldish woman with untidy grey hair. Oh mother, mother, she sighed, wiping spots of toothpaste from the glass, making the image blur. What did you ever seek to teach me, other than curling my hair, and pie frills, other than dusting, making beds, and keeping my knees and lips tight together?

Edith had always found it hard to believe in her mother's faith, her absolute conviction that she was doing the right thing. Edith could have understood it if her mother had been happy, and now wanted her daughter to be happy too. But Mrs Johnson's view of married life was almost entirely negative. It was a question of putting up with things, mostly. As a young girl Edith had not been won over by the prospect, and she found domestic activities boring. She quite liked using the pink lipstick Mrs Johnson bought her when she was almost seventeen, but thought the boys who escorted her to and from school dances, usually wishing for a goodnight kiss on the doorstep, were boring too.

Now she knew why she had come into the bathroom: to get rid of the pharmaceutical clutter her mother had left behind, bottles, tubes, the half empty packs of pills. She was holding a rubbish bag in her left hand, big enough to take the lot, including even the bedpan Mrs Johnson had been using for this past year. Edith went to the bathroom shelf but found she could not distinguish the labels, hers from her mother's, things she might still need. Her eyes were suddenly swimming in tears, and she was crying helplessly, like a child. It was so unfair, she thought, sniffing back the tears. It was not as though she expected gratitude. It was not even that she had willingly turned her back on wedded bliss, far from it. Loneliness had chosen her in the end, not the other way round.

What a relief, she thought, trying to cheer herself up, as the bedpan thumped into the gaping mouth of the rubbish bag. No more of mother's daily shit, laughing without much humour, recalling the disgust she was never able quite to overcome when she took the bedpan from under her mother. She had been ashamed of this feeling, this revulsion, which did not lessen over the months.

She could have borne it, she often thought, but for Robert. If she had not also had to listen to the fulsome eulogies, mostly in the presence of visitors, of her dear brother Robert, his wife, his money, the size of his well-appointed house. Even in the absence of others Mrs Johnson seemed to have completely erased all memory of the events which had brought her to these draughty, shabby rooms she disliked so much. I could never win, thought Edith, fumbling in the kitchen drawer for string, then tying the mouth of the bulging bag with a viciously tight knot. It was always him, never me. It would have been better for me if I had stopped trying long ago.

Edith bumped the rubbish bag down the two flights of

stairs to the dustbin area at the side of the house. Lingering for a moment, she took deep breaths of the spring air, saw how a bird flitted across her vision, how clear the sky was high overhead. Suddenly she had all the time in the world. It was a bit overwhelming. Robert would have to be told, but not now. She would have to do something about her mother's room, but it could wait.

Hearing the laughter of children behind her, Edith climbed the flight of steps to the heavy main door. As she got to her own landing her spirit sank, grew heavy as lead. The truth was, now that her own life had been given back to her, she did not know what to do with it, how to occupy the hours and days ahead. She could hear birdsong just behind the windows, but around her loomed empty space, silence and shadows, rooms waiting to be re-inhabited, redefined in some as yet unspecified manner. It was a relief, but also frightening. For so long she had been strung along by duty: do this, that, fetch and carry, lift me, turn me, plump my pillows, fetch my other cardigan. How to pick up the threads of her own life? What was her life, now that she was by herself?

Edith stood in the hallway and tried to remember what it had been like, all those years ago, before mother had moved in. But she had still been working then; for five days out of seven she did not have to think about what to do, how to occupy the hours, and the weekend served as a welcome respite, over far too quickly. Standing at the door of her mother's room, staring in at the empty bed, the slight dip in the mattress, the mound of bedding at the lower end, Edith suspected that there was no thread. She had become, mentally and physically, certainly in the eyes of the world, a different person.

This was utterly disorientating. Until now Edith simply had not had a moment in which to consider herself, what she would do after her mother went. It was not just that Mrs Johnson needed so much looking after, she had a way of filling up every nook and cranny of the day, of every waking second, until her secret self, the individual she had nurtured since childhood, seemed to have been crushed. Once, before Mrs Johnson moved in, she had been capable of living by herself, for herself, in ways she found satisfying. She had known how to fill her days with minor purposes and pleasures. In fact, Edith suspected that it was this ability which Mrs Johnson found so impossible to forgive, which got increasingly under her skin, so she was hellbent on destroying it. To see Edith living contentedly, despite her failure to find a husband, was intolerable.

Edith had wandered aimlessly into the living room. Dropping into a chair, she stared out of the window. A little white cloud was drifting over the rooftops. A large bird sat on a chimneypot, settling its wings. Edith had been a difficult, rebellious child, from Mrs Johnson's point of view, and had not mended her ways in adulthood. You might say she was now paying the price. And so she referred to her as poor Edith, embarrassing her in front of the few friends loyal enough to continue visiting, despite the trying, overbearing presence of her mother. Poor Edith had missed the bus, had not known, as she herself had, however briefly, the contentment, the natural fulfil-ment of matrimony. It had been hard, whilst still relatively young, to find herself a war widow, but at least she had the memory of a few happy years as a wife and mother. Poor Edith, on the other hand, even though living in more stable times, had been unable to achieve this goal, having, she would add confidentially, failed to maximise her natural assets. Not that Edith was ever a great beauty, but she could look pleasing on occasion, when she made the effort. The fact that she herself had never laid claims to exceptional looks underlined, by contrast, her own success.

The bird on the chimneypot flew off. Edith looked round the large, shabby room, the setting for so many such scenes. Perhaps her mother could not forgive her daughter for what Robert had done to bring her to this dependence. And so she had to triumph, to turn her humiliation round by brandishing a spurious cup of victory. She had been a married woman, and her daughter had not. Perhaps, too, she was getting her own back for Edith's sulky adolescence, for saying it was unfair that her brother Robert never had to wash up or peel potatoes, for refusing to wear the girdle, for, above all, getting such good school reports. The fact that Edith's teachers thought highly of her, putting, moreover, nonsensical ideas into her head about further education, had been an outrage to Mrs Johnson, who had left school at fourteen, and who felt that, if anyone did well at school, it ought to be the boy of the family. But no teacher ever wrote or said nice things about Robert. Lazy, could do better, here in body but not in spirit, such remarks were the norm. And so, thought Edith, she had this continuing compulsion to get her own back, by harping on what she saw as Edith's shortcomings, attempting to elevate her own status by putting Edith down. She might speak sorrowfully in public, but the occasional unprovoked remark, spiteful as a poisoned dart, spoke of inner resentment.

It was perhaps for this reason, to emphasise her

superior status, that Mrs Johnson had insisted, when she moved in with Edith, that the framed photograph of her dead husband should stand prominently displayed in the living room, Edith's living room. Edith, who had almost no memory of her father, felt uneasy about it. She was staring at it now. A youthful face, blank, blandly smiling, inside his crisp uniform. It was a studio photograph, head and shoulders against a white background, deliberately posed to show off the uniform. Even his features were somehow uniform, as though conforming to old-fashioned ideals no longer in fashion. All over the country there must have been similar young men having their pictures taken before going off to war.

Growing up in the post-war years, this picture had been almost an icon for young Edith. The smiling features had taken on the characteristics of what might have been, if her father had lived. He was a missing god, the protecting presence who would have made sure she got justice in the world, starting within her mother's house. He would have shielded her from her mother's wrath, and been impervious both to Robert's boyish charm and the terror of his tantrums. That, at least, was the tenor of her secret dream, the love she had for an unknown father. Otherwise she had only the fragmentary and vague memories which are part of early childhood, recollections belied by the image so prominent on the mantelpiece.

Looking at the familiar picture, now that the face had become so impossibly youthful, Edith knew she might have been harbouring an illusion. But she had not been altogether wrong to hanker for him. Fathers were known to favour their daughters, as mothers were beguiled by a son. He would have balanced the scales, and she would have been daddy's girl, worn her femininity lightly, joyously, like a party frock. Not a dreary shift, not sackcloth.

Perhaps it was only the uniform made him a hero. Nevertheless a man, a man of the world, would have seen through him, not been so gullible. Right from the start he would have insisted that his son embark on a proper profession, acquiring the necessary qualifications first. He would have recognised, as her mother had not, that Robert was getting his schooling, not in the classroom, but elsewhere. Any man of principle, knowing the world, would have put a stop to it.

Edith had seen, from the beginning, how her mother had been rendered blind by lack of knowledge, not simply too much affection. He had begun his extracurricular activities whilst still in primary school, his knees grubby, his short trousers bulging at the pockets when he returned from school. Out he would bring his peculiar, unfamiliar booty, coins, pencil sharpeners, a whistle, even a dog's tooth once, the result of that day's barter. His system was simple: he did not mind what he acquired, so long as he thought he was getting more for less, since almost everything was used for further barter. He had no desires in the playground, except to play on the desires of others. And so, when he did exchange more for less, apparently, he did so knowingly, knowing precisely which child had been eyeing a small knife with envy, a milky marble with lust. He might set off in the morning with a single horse chestnut in his pocket, knowing that half the playground had been eyeing it for days, hypnotised by its history, spellbound by its record of invincibility. Or a single card, required by a particular boy to complete a set, thus increasing its value sevenfold. He had known when he got it, apparently bartering over the odds, who would give almost anything for it. Robert had few playthings, but his tin money box got increasingly heavy. He had grandiose plans for the future, when he was grown up, for which he was saving.

Mrs Johnson had been amused by his childish cunning. It seemed harmless enough. She allowed him to run wild, saying that boys will be boys, as he scampered about the streets, got grubby knees and tore his trousers. Whilst Robert lost his homework and brought home rubbish from vacant lots, Edith took on the responsibility of her girlhood. She did the washing-up, sewed on buttons, was kept back from school when Mrs Johnson got a bad attack of influenza. It was hard catching up at school, but harder still to win her mother's approval. If she did things right her conduct provoked no comment, only when she burnt the potatoes or forgot to buy sugar on the way back from school, then Mrs Johnson would speak at some length of her shortcomings.

Edith still felt a dull ache under her ribs when she remembered those final, painful years in her mother's house. Robert could do no wrong, whilst she could do nothing right, or not enough. But you were absent, she said out loud to her father's picture, falling back on this habit of her childhood, when she had communed secretly with this icon in its tarnished frame, appealing for justice, spilling out her heartache. Then, as now, her mother had kept the black and white photograph of her husband, missing in action, presumed dead, in a prominent position in the living room. After vigorously rubbing the glass and frame with a duster Mrs Johnson always put it back at a very specific angle. It continued to stand in the front room when the war ended, when other men were coming back to their old jobs and Mrs Johnson went to work in the shoe shop, and when Robert had begun to fill up the rest of the house with odd and unpredictable merchandise, trading on post-war shortages, on any deal he could find.

Wearily, Edith got up and walked across the room to peer more closely at her father's face. Not a spot, not a blemish; presumably the studios did a lot of touching up in those days. In the end she had left, giving up all thought of further education, simply to get away. Robert, having left school at the earliest opportunity, continued to live at home whilst he embarked on his dubious career of underhand trading. During this youthful hand-to-mouth existence, constantly out of funds, he came and went at will, using the rooms, using his mother too.

Edith took her father's picture to her mother's empty room and put it in a drawer, on top of an untidy heap of underwear. She did not want to touch the clothing, not yet. She pushed the drawer shut and went to the window, lifting the lower sash as high as it would go. Outside a grey cat slunk across the pitted lawn, stalking a small bird pecking for worms. But the bird fluttered up into a nearby tree by an easy margin. Sniffing the spring air as it blew in, the odour of blossom and grass, her mind was not on the present scene, but sifting through far-off rubbish, layers of detritus left behind long ago, but not forgotten. Perhaps not left behind, after all.

The cat was now sharpening its claws on the tree trunk, but the bird had flown. A cloud of new green hung in the branches of every tree. Edith saw the small house filling up with Robert's goods, bought speculatively. He had not made so much as a token effort to find a job. The starting salary was always too low, the prospects unpromising. So he brought back cardboard boxes full of goods bought in bulk: men's shirts, or tennis shoes, or cheap china ornaments. Goods would block the hallway, the upstairs landing. Once Edith could not get into her room because it was filled with collapsible stepladders, on another occasion it was cluttered up with electric kettles. It was usual for the top of Mrs Johnson's wardrobe to be stacked to the ceiling with unwanted goods which had so far failed to find a ready market. Mrs Johnson said that Robert had to start somewhere, that Edith was just being selfish. It might be a bit difficult to get into the bathroom, or even her own room, but it was only temporary, hardly worth fussing about.

Edith took to doing her homework elsewhere, in the public library or at the home of a schoolfriend. If she was lucky her friend's mother would invite her to stay for supper. She had outgrown her winter coat, but Mrs Johnson said they could not afford a new one this year. Shortly afterwards Edith found out that her mother had paid for a gross of electric toasters, Robert having cash flow problems. He had, it seems, been threatened. Mrs Johnson began to economise in other ways, and they no longer had roast beef on Sunday, only sausages or shepherd's pie. Nobody bought the toasters.

Finding it impossible to argue about what was happening, Edith finally left. As far as her son was concerned, Mrs Johnson's indulgence knew no bounds, and she was blind to his shortcomings. The discussions with Edith simply got acrimonious. So she had left, giving up any notion of studying at the university. Thinking it would be easier, by now wishing only to be free, independent, to put a space between herself and her mother, her brother too. But it was only a breathing space, as it turned out. She should have continued fighting, arguing.

Edith, leaning on the windowsill, heard two plump wood pigeons burbling their deep and curious song. She thought bitterly of this, how she had lost out in the end, with her mother's continuing folly. Mrs Johnson would not see the error of her ways, or Robert for what he was and had always been. Even after the final catastrophe, even after she had to move in with Edith as a consequence, she managed a kind of total forgetfulness on the subject, or rather, a selective memory, false, self-deceiving, which enabled her to think and speak just as she had before.

At first, after she had moved in, they had both kept silent. Edith had thought it tactful, and did not wish to hurt her mother unnecessarily. This went on for several weeks. Then, quite suddenly, Edith overheard Mrs Johnson telling a friend of hers, a woman who used to work in the same office and still kept in touch with Edith, how successful her son was in business, owning a detached house with half an acre of ground and a double garage in a very good neighbourhood. Her voice died away when Edith brought the tea tray into the living room, but from that day forward Mrs Johnson gained in assurance, and could be relied upon to make it a regular topic in front of visitors, whether Edith was listening or not.

Mostly she would expatiate on his present prosperity, the Georgian house, newly built, needless to say, with everything just so; but occasionally she might, to high-light his enterprising spirit, speak of his early days, how hard it had been for him, since she was a war widow and unable to give him a proper start in life. It seems she had completely forgotten the life insurance she had cashed in for Robert, early on, to get him out of serious trouble. Edith, who had not forgotten, kept silent, but her hand would begin to shake over the tea things, so the cups rattled too loudly in their saucers. It was a relief, from this point of view, when her mother became bedridden and could no longer queen it over the living room.

A hard way to think of it, but it was necessary to be truthful, now that the bed behind her was empty, now that this space was hers once more, only hers. She had expended so much energy on trying to win her mother, smoothing the rough, turning a blind eye, a deaf ear to the constant barbs, too much salt in the soup, not enough onions in the stew, but Robert, oh Robert. Spinning a laborious cobweb to disguise old wounds. And it had been hopeless from the beginning. But it was only by fooling herself that she could do the right thing, what she knew to be her duty. Perhaps it was this that made her mother so cruel, the sharp remarks so unrelenting. Edith was letting herself go, had put on weight, should get her hair seen to. No. Edith was being dutiful, too good. And Mrs Johnson could not stand being in her debt.

It was necessary at this juncture to see clearly, if she was to go on. Edith had turned away from the window and was confronted by the unmade bed, blankets pulled back, battered pillows, the hollow down the middle of the mattress. She hung the blankets across the sill of the open window, hoping the fresh spring wind would get rid of the odour.

She should have known, after her mother cashed in her insurance policy, how it would end. Perhaps, deep down, she had always known that something of the kind might happen, but had felt powerless to alter the course of events. And then, she thought, watching a grey squirrel scamper over the garden fence, she, not just her mother, had been lulled into a false sense of security by Robert's rise in the world. Robert now had an expensive, flashy motor car and an expensive, flashy wife to go with it. He still bought and sold, but much more mysteriously. Cheap items in cardboard boxes were a thing of the past. Edith almost never saw him, but when she took tea with her mother on Sundays Mrs Johnson spoke vaguely of business dealings involving blocks of flats, a sports stadium, even an entire shopping complex up in the north.

Mrs Johnson told her that Robert was part of a consortium, though neither of them really knew what the word meant. But Mrs Johnson was impressed by the word, as she was always impressed by Robert and what he had to tell her. Mrs Johnson told her that Robert was into a new partnership, and that Marilyn had a new fur coat. Mrs Johnson did not tell her daughter that she had signed away her house, no doubt thinking it a mere formality, given her son's prosperity. The first Edith knew about it was when she went to visit her mother in the hospital after she had her stroke, brought on by the shock of learning that her son could not meet his debts and her house would have to be sold. Even then she did not learn of it directly, since her mother was half paralysed and had, for the moment, lost her power of speech. She made a slow, stubborn recovery, from wheelchair to stick, from speechlessness to broken sentences. By the time she was well enough to move into her daughter's flat the entire episode seemed to have been erased from her mind.

. 2 .

What to do with this room, now it was so very empty?

Edith went into the living room and opened the upright piano, which had stood neglected for so long. It was badly in need of tuning, and her hands felt stiff, the fingers intent on stumbling over each other. Edith wondered whether she might begin again, now that she had the rooms to herself, and more leisure. Mrs Johnson had disliked the noise from the moment she moved in, and found unending pretexts to interrupt, bring her playing to an end. Edith had given up even before her mother became bedbound, endlessly demanding, constantly querulous. She had lost heart, too timid to interrupt the underlying stillness.

But now . . . well, all in good time. She got up from the piano stool and stood at the window for a moment. A great day to be young, she found herself thinking, seeing figures below pass by in bright spring clothing, sunlight touching old brickwork and new leaf. Edith thought she would have a cup of tea and was on her way to the kitchen when she heard a knock at the door.

Standing stock-still in the dim hallway, she held her breath, listening. No sound, but the shadow of what might perhaps be two feet under the door, swaying slightly. Or might be just the shadows of leaves stirring beyond, interrupting the light. She was suddenly jumpy, on her own now, alert to the unexpected. But she opened the door.

On her threshold stood Martha Wolf, a person Edith did not know, and thought of as not quite real. Rhoda, who lived next door to them on the floor below, had dubbed the Wolfs 'the ghosts', and the term had stuck. Both of them were heard rather than seen, and then only briefly, at dusk or early dawn, flitting hastily out of peripheral vision. The two kept themselves to themselves, and Edith, respecting this wish, had taken to averting her eyes when she did catch a glimpse of one or both.

But here she now stood, looking straight at her. Edith was struck dumb by the look, the two dark eyes focusing on hers. It was like looking into a black abyss, a bottomless pit. The rest of her, skin and hair, the wool clothing clinging loosely to her thin limbs, had a uniformly grey and dusty look, dry, as if she had stopped ageing years ago.

I saw how they took your mother away.

Each syllable was pronounced with the precision peculiar to foreigners, but softly.

I hope this is not a bad time? But I felt I had to come up to you.

Edith, who had been staring speechlessly, shook herself out of her stupor and stepped back.

No. Of course not.

Martha Wolf stepped through the door as though she had been doing it for years, leading Edith into the front room.

Losing a mother is a dreadful thing.

She was looking round the room with curiosity, then back at Edith.

But I know you did all you could for her, for as long as you could. That must be a great comfort.

Edith shrugged uneasily, motioned her visitor to sit down.

I have no such comfort. I lost my mother in early youth.

She had been sitting forward in her chair, stroking the long fingers of her left hand with the thumb of her right hand, up and down. Now she looked at Edith.

Perhaps you do not know, how could you, but I lost my mother in such a way that I must feel guilty. It is not rational, but I cannot help it. We do not speak of it, but I know we both suffer, and will continue to do so.

Edith, listening intently, felt it best to say nothing. Martha Wolf's nervous intensity was compelling.

That is why I have found it in my soul to envy you. Forgive me, I did not wish to pry, but I could hear you, tending to her wants at all hours of the day and night, and my heart was bursting. You will, I think, find it a comfort, in the years ahead, to know you did all you could for a person so dear to you.

She leaned forward and touched her briefly on the wrist in a consoling gesture. Edith had a devilish impulse to laugh. It would have been a harsh, humourless outburst but, sensing her visitor's deeply felt sincerity, she suppressed it.

Can I offer you a cup of tea?

Martha Wolf shook her head. Edith was thinking how odd it was, for years she had been overhearing sounds from the rooms below, hoping to find out about such mysterious neighbours, foreign and withdrawn. They moved about quietly, almost stealthily, and she did not hear much. Now she found that Martha Wolf had also been listening. How absurd it was, and whose fault?

I think my brother feels her loss even more deeply, though he says nothing. It is because, all these years we have been living together, he does not choose to speak of her, of her death, that I know how bad it is for him.

So, another small mystery finally solved. They shared a common surname, that much was known. But prying at their incoming post and eavesdropping on sounds coming through the walls had not been enough to establish their precise relationship, which had been puzzling the neighbours for years.

You see, we left our country together, under very difficult circumstances. By the skin of our teeth. Our mother was the first to say: you must go. I try to remember this, when I dream of her in the night. And then it was Frederick who was most at risk, in the early days. They had been arresting the young men, and on occasion beating them up in broad daylight, on the streets.

Martha Wolf was looking intently at Edith, as though only she could set her free from the horror of her youth, by taking it in fully. Edith felt she was hearing the plot of a film, black and white, alien, but she attempted to look as though she understood.

We left with nothing, when we did go. Just the clothes we stood up in. Two weeks before they broke down the door of our apartment, our mother's apartment, and set about systematically destroying everything. They had axes, weapons. Glass was broken, chairs and tables hacked apart, books torn, curtains and pictures ripped from the walls. I do not know why they did not kill me or my mother, since they might have done so with impunity. I think perhaps they just enjoyed our terror.

My God.

Edith felt utterly foolish, hearing herself. She thought she knew about this kind of thing, but listening to this living, breathing person made everything different. Nor did she know what kind of God, if any, Martha Wolf obeyed. The last thing she wished to do was impinge on religious sensibility.

Gesindel.

Edith could not make out the foreign word, but her visitor was glaring with sudden ferocity. She shook slightly too, holding on to the arms of the chair for support.

Frederick was out. He did not come back for hours, so we thought perhaps he would not return. You see, we knew of so many friends who had been put into a camp. But he had simply been hiding until the uproar, the looting and breaking, died off. It was next morning that our mother made us swear that we would get out of the country at the first opportunity. We had permits, you see; many of our friends were not so lucky. Visas to almost any country in the world were hard to get, but we had been hesitating, not just on account of the uncertainty of our future in a foreign country. Our mother was also in our thoughts. Older persons, especially those in poor health, were seldom accepted in a foreign country, and so far she had been unsuccessful. But now she begged us to go.

23

Martha was looking at her with those dark, cavernous eyes, but had stopped speaking. She seemed to have difficulty in breathing, and a rather prominent Adam's apple in her longish neck was moving up and down, as if she were swallowing her words, which kept rising.

It must have been hard for her. Edith felt she had to help her along. Hard for all of you. But she was right, clearly.

Our mother came to the railway station when we left. I have a recurring dream about it, just as it was. A bit of smut got in her eye as we were beginning to move. She wore a brown fur coat. I could see it even though her face was just a blur. We received a few letters from her, after we arrived in this country. The last was from a relative, telling us she had committed suicide when the order came to assemble the following morning.

The two women sat on in the stillness, unmoving. Edith felt that anything she might say would be worse than unavailing. She could hear a clock ticking, her own breathing. She knew that Martha Wolf coming now, speaking out now, after years of hiding, had not been done lightly. She felt unworthy of such a gift.

· 3 ·

Edith had slept fitfully, and shuffled off to the kitchen with aching limbs, her mind a grey fog. First thing in the morning she often had serious doubts about living, and had learnt to suspend judgement until after her first cup of tea. I'm still here, she would think, staring blearily at a sky without prospects, feeling her ageing body clinging on.

It was best simply to get on with it. Holding the kettle over the sink, Edith turned the cold tap, but nothing issued from it, other than a hollow gurgling. The water supply was off, had probably been off most of the night. This was happening too frequently, she thought crossly, remembering previous interruptions recently, though they were usually only for an hour or two. Living on the top floor, she was the first tenant to go without. And the interruptions were getting more lengthy: only a fortnight ago she had been without water from mid-afternoon until the following morning. Edith let out her annoyance by thumping the kettle hard on the gas ring, and went off to get dressed.

Beyond her window she saw a high, tender sky, without limit, and swifts dipping and diving freely, as if in utter joy. But she herself felt trapped by the unexpected, could not relish this morning whilst things were not proceeding as they should. Edith knew she was wasting her time, but nevertheless felt a niggling compulsion to exert herself, to do her utmost to put things right. So she began ringing the water authority's emergency number, only to find it constantly engaged. She kept moving restlessly from room to room between such attempts. She told herself the entire district must be without water, hence the busy line, but though this should have been reassuring, knowing everybody was in the same situation, it did not prevent her from trying yet again.

The sun was continuing its spring arc into the sky. Edith quenched her thirst with milk, but went on feeling thirsty. Down below she could see people sauntering up and down the road in the sunlight, wearing bright clothing. Blossom blew from the trees like wedding confetti, moving in thick drifts on the pavement. Edith found herself looking down with envy, as if she was trapped, by her thirst, by her smelly, unwashed body.

She kept trying the tap, trying the telephone. Her mouth felt so unpleasant from the milk, which she did not usually drink, that she went to the living room for the sherry bottle, even though it was still morning, much too early for a tipple. It did nothing for her thirst, but a consoling warmth spread stealthily through her, and she began to relax. There was nothing, after all, she could do, no amount of tap turning would bring back the supply a moment sooner, it just added to her frustration. Sinking back in her armchair, she gazed out at a flock of milky clouds floating over the rooftops.

Feeling slightly dizzy, Edith did try for further information. Now she got a pretty little tune, followed by a recorded message, telling her she would be dealt with in strict rotation. Or try later, said the voice. Half an hour later a recording told her the supply would be restored as soon as possible.

Meanwhile dirty dishes had begun to pile up in the sink, whilst the spirit level in her sherry bottle sank. The sun had risen to its apogee, scaled the roof and was sinking down on the other side. Now it was slanting through the topmost branches of trees which had stood for a century, reaching to the sky. The light moving round her feet on the old mousy carpet was a dancing rivulet, a pool, with its moving shadows of leaf, branch and cloud. Far away the sound of schoolchildren on their way home, their bright chatter drifting in on the wind.

Spring, thought Edith, watching the pool of light, the shadows of leaf stirring near her foot. Such a glorious beginning, this dazzling pattern. There was a dark stain on the carpet, where she had accidentally knocked over the sherry glass, but she could not summon up enough energy to get out of her chair. No water to clean up anyhow, and the carpet was worn out. Everything here was old, worn out and ugly. Nothing she could do about it. But for the river of spring sunlight, and new leaf stirring. But for the singing voices of children, dancing on the wind.

She did not know how long she had been sitting in this fashion, swimming in a blur of sensory impressions, letting herself go, there being nothing else for her to do, nowhere to go, only that she had lost all feeling for the mandatory clock ticking, issuing unending orders. The knock on the door seemed to come from far off to reach her, and she was slow to respond. She got out of the chair with difficulty, hauling herself up from the sunken springs.

On the threshold stood Chris, young Chris, his blonde hair a halo of light. She perceived him and his halo through a sudden upsurge of tears in which the vision of him lost definition. She had been sitting too long, doing nothing, and sherry made her sentimental.

Mum said to give you a hand. He was mumbling, shifting uneasily on the landing, from left foot to right. It was as though he did not know her, now that he had grown so much this past year or two. Awkward and shy, he stood self-consciously, not looking at her directly. Edith, remembering how he would run up the stairs, into her arms, shrill words tumbling out of him, felt a dull pain under her ribs, and helpless tears welling over.

Mum said to give you a hand, he had said. There's a water lorry down in the road.

Oh Chris, she sighed, her head still swimming slightly with alcohol. You are so good to me.

Together they searched out a couple of buckets and when he returned up the stairs to pour water into the biggest of her saucepans she was able to stroke him, touch his thick fair hair as she did when he was small. She saw how he flushed, and though she told herself the spreading colour was due to exertion the dull pain under her ribs was back with renewed force. Only a few years ago he had squealed with delight if she tickled him, cuddling him on her lap, playing round and round the garden.

I'll bring up a bit more, muttered Chris, avoiding her eyes. Mum said not to drink it, but to boil it first.

But it was his mother who was good to her, had always been so, ever since Edith had known her. And it was Jane who had taught her son to be thoughtful as he was growing, do things for others. If Edith had been able to help out, she had been only too glad to do so. Watching the boy leap down the staircase, swinging an empty bucket in each hand, Edith knew how much joy it had given her, minding the boy for an hour whilst his mother went on an errand.

She had been glad to help out, knowing how hard it was for a mother, working, on her own. She could see him even now, stubby legs struggling up the steep stairs, clutching a sprig of mint. Mummy grew it in the garden.

Chris came up the stairs a second time, panting with effort. He rested the buckets on the last landing, then brought them up the final flight to her door.

Mum said to mind your back.

I will.

It was good of his mother to remember about her back. Lifting anything heavy could put it out, and Jane would often offer to help with Mrs Johnson, when the old lady became bedbound. Edith stood on the threshold now, wanting to hold him back, just a little longer, knowing the days when she could beguile him with a biscuit, hold his attention with an old photograph album, were past. She stood, watching his bright hair bob down the stairwell. He felt free, now his duty was done.

She shut the door slowly, with a sigh. He must go. Old Mrs Johnson never knew this, and frightened him off. If he was sent up on an errand she had a habit of calling out to him from the bedroom, to ask him about school. Chris, being a polite child, would go into her room unwillingly, obviously bothered by the sick room, the sight of her in bed. Let him be, she had told her mother, who had not understood, thought it good to take an interest in him, basking in her own kindliness.

Edith set water on the stove, and stood by the window, waiting for it to boil. An afterglow, pink and gold, lit up the sky beyond the rooftops, blackly outlining the chimneypots, a bird settling its feathers. She was glad to see the day dying, if in glory.

· 4 ·

Edith had difficulty waking up, now that she was by herself. It was a slow process, resembling the blind fumbling of a crablike creature inhabiting an alien shell. First a sensory exploration of the housing in which she was held, her body, for signs of discomfort. Then a confrontation of the existential vacuum beyond. It still felt like a vacuum, that was her problem. When her mother was in the next room Edith was usually woken abruptly, a cry for attention would bring her round, and she was up and about without a moment of prior thought. Now there was no such imperative.

Edith attempted to crawl back through the curtain of sleep, to find the interior logic of her dream. She had intended to visit her mother, had been searching the streets for a bunch of pink tulips, but could not find a florist, nor a flower stall. She no longer knew why she could not go empty-handed, nor why only tulips would do. The curtain was fading, turning a pallid grey.

She could not shut her eyes to the daylight.

And then the body makes its own demands, overruling all else. Absently, Edith padded into the bathroom. It was only when she could not flush, when she saw the heap of laundry under the washbasin, that she remembered. The taps, when she turned them, emitted only a hollow death rattle. Utter despondency swept over her. She would simply have to go on coping, there being no sign of a return to normality.

Gradually, as she got going, indignation provided a spurt of energy. She had to think ahead, constantly, plan minor tasks which she usually did with her mind elsewhere. It must have been like this for our ancestors, she thought, surviving by the hour, everything a challenge. No vacuum now. As soon as her mind started to drift a reflex action would pull her back to present reality. It was so easy, so completely automatic, turning on the tap. And now: nothing.

Laboriously, Edith washed, restored her self-respect, did the dirty dishes stacked in the sink. Having used up her emergency supply, she set off down the flight of stairs with bucket and kettle to fetch more water. A bright sky beyond the high window was cheering: she would not, at least, need to fetch and carry in wind and rain.

On the first-floor landing she met nobody. Rhoda was away, and the Wolfs still kept very much to themselves. Although Martha had become slightly less retiring: yesterday she had exchanged a few words about the water crisis, if nervously. It was as if both of them were anxious to build on the contact which had at long last been established, but did not know how to proceed. Edith, conscious of Martha Wolf's timidity, a reclusive instinct verging on compulsion, did not wish to seem pushy, and so held back, leaving Martha to take the initiative. Whilst the latter might have been looking for an invitation she did not get. Edith did however ask whether the Wolfs had sufficient buckets, and so forth, and received a shy smile on offering to lend them extra receptacles. She felt as if they were both swaying on a flimsy rope bridge, high above an abyss.

Inevitably, Mrs Gardiner was lying in wait for her in the hall. Smartly dressed despite the early hour, she stood, firm as a rock, on her threshold, beige cashmere clinging to her bulky hips and ample bosom, crisply groomed hair firm as a helmet, fingering a brooch pinned to the silk cravat of her blouse.

I don't know what this country is coming to, she stated firmly.

Edith had heard this sort of remark too regularly to respond. In the past she occasionally pretended to agree with her, in a vague fashion, to avoid a lengthy argument which would, she knew, be utterly pointless. It was no good telling Mrs Gardiner that existence had always been a chancy business throughout history, in this country too, for most of its inhabitants. She was deaf to any such suggestion. She knew whom to blame, and for what, and stuck rigidly to her own opinion.

Things were never like this in the old days.

Edith, anxious to find the water lorry, could think only of trying to find a way round her neighbour, who was blocking her path. Mrs Gardiner had a vision of the old days quite unlike anything Edith could recall, nor did it altogether tally with what her own mother had told her.

We have a right to expect a reliable service. I shall

write to the water authority. I have a relative who is very high up in the civil service. I shall write to him.

Hardly worth it. Edith tried to sound soothing, though still bent on cutting conversation short. No doubt the supply will be back in an hour or two, at worst by the end of the day.

You think so? The charges keep rising, and we get nothing for it. And now my cleaning woman has let me down. She says she is ill, but I think she is lying. You can't trust anybody these days, and I do not trust her. If I did not watch her she would not dust properly, missing out the nooks and crannies, not lifting ornaments. I have to spend all my time watching her, otherwise it is hardly worth paying her. Perhaps it is not worth paying her. And now she is demanding more pay as from next month or, she says, she will cease coming. I do not know what to do. But she does not steal things, nor does she drink. I once had a woman whose breath smelled very bad, of liquor, and who was totally untrustworthy. I had to get rid of her, whereupon she got vehemently abusive.

Mrs Gardiner was staring at her with startled eyes, as though the shock had not yet subsided.

Yes, well, Edith muttered lamely. She found Mrs Gardiner's attitude to the lower classes distinctly embarrassing. Then, determined to make her escape, she added: I'm going to fill up at the water lorry.

It's not there! The triumph in her voice was unmistakable. All her worst predictions were being confirmed. Go and look, if you don't believe me.

And she made way for Edith, her bucket and tin kettle. Edith hurriedly went through the front door, feeling crestfallen, her smug sense of moral superiority dying away rapidly, to be replaced by anxiety.

Outside she saw no sign of a water lorry. Only several figures standing uncertainly, the length of the pavement, with buckets or other containers. Clouds had begun scudding across the rooftops, and a teasing wind was tossing bits of rubbish upward, also swirls of dying blossom.

A woman standing nearby approached.

I'm told they are going to put up standpipes.

She spoke glumly, and Edith's spirit sank. The woman was unknown to her, as were the other individuals further down. An atmosphere of indecision hung round them, momentum suspended, as though held in limbo. Edith could sense this paralysis of will affecting her too, standing in the wind, staring down an empty road.

Who told you this?

She was wary of rumour, truth being the first casualty in an emergency.

That man.

The woman pointed the spout of her kettle towards a bald man standing a few yards further down.

He was down here earlier, so he says. Spoke to a workman who left. That's all I know.

Nobody can get through for information.

Doubtfully, Edith assessed the man with the bald head, but did not go up to him. He was standing in shirtsleeves, now and then jiggling up and down on his heels. When sunlight appeared fitfully through the clouds his bald pate gleamed like a varnished wooden egg.

But now a gust of wind blew through her, and Edith felt cold.

35

I think it's going to rain, she said, turning to climb up the front flight of steps.

Mrs Gardiner was standing at her bay window, peering through the net curtains. She was always watching, spying on comings and goings, apparently under the delusion that she was not seen. When Edith glanced in her direction she hastily withdrew.

Halfway through the morning two men could be seen outside the house, raising a paving stone, then fixing a standpipe. Edith, who had been to the shops for fresh food, did not know whether to be relieved or annoyed at the sight. The standpipe had an air of permanency about it, which was disturbing. But at least there would be water of a sort. It seemed that the entire street was affected, for she saw the men crossing the road to lift another paving stone with their tools, and when she went down with her bucket she saw several more standpipes at intervals down the length of the street. But the reason for this disruption was still a mystery, since the authority was not answering telephone callers. When Edith attempted to get through she either got a busy signal or an unending ringing sound, as though the office had shut down.

In the absence of reliable news, people paused to exchange rumours whilst waiting their turn round the standpipes. An elderly woman had heard from a neighbour, who had actually spoken to the workmen erecting the standpipes, that a water main had burst half a mile away. But nobody had seen flooding. Later in the day Edith was told by an adolescent boy, who had heard it at school, that a terrorist plot to poison the water supply had been uncovered at the eleventh hour. Mrs Gardiner, standing regally at the top of the flight of steps, watching Edith struggle with yet another heavy bucket, told her of unofficial strike action, and union sabotage. She had it on good authority, the mother of her relative in the civil service, with whom she had just been in touch.

Edith, struggling up the two flights of stairs with the slopping water, was past caring about the truth behind it. Her shoulders were aching, she kept having to put down her burden, and each time she lifted it once more the water seemed to be heavier than a moment ago. Her calf muscles hurt too, and by the time she reached her front door she was gasping for breath. Spots swam through her vision, and she had to sit down rather hastily.

When she got her breath back and her vision cleared she saw what a mess she was now living in. There were rings of water on the floors, little puddles which had turned muddy from walking through them. The bathroom was full of dirty linen, the kitchen stacked high with unwashed pots and pans. Most of all she longed to soak in a hot bath.

Instead, Edith took herself down to the basement flat. Jane always made her welcome, offered her tea, a hot meal now and then and, most important of all, a listening ear. Edith knew nobody else with whom she could unwind, disgorge pent-up emotions, dismiss anxieties, and simply feel warmly human. Whilst Mrs Johnson was living with her she had, now and then, found it essential to get away for an hour, in order to keep an even temper, to prevent an involuntary outburst. To circumvent such a loss of control she would hurry down, using a flimsy pretext, anything.

Afterwards, putting water on to boil first thing in the morning, Edith felt she had perhaps been indiscreet, and put it down to excessive fatigue, all this stress. Neverthe-less, she felt it was perhaps verging on disloyalty to have told Jane of the financial catastrophe which led to her mother moving into the flat, and of the resentment she felt against her brother. Until now she had never breathed a word to suggest that Mrs Johnson's residence with her had not been freely decided by both of them.

But now it was out, and she did not know whether she was glad or sorry. Perhaps it did not matter, not now, and she knew Jane did not go round gossiping, she had too much to do, for a start, to indulge in such behaviour. Peering out of her kitchen window, Edith could see the by now usual crowd of people queueing up for the standpipe down below. Curiosity kept her rather longer at the window when she saw Fred Wolf standing in line. It was unusual to catch even a glimpse of him, so she made the most of her opportunity now.

He stood down there, half a head taller than anybody else in the line, as though by an act of will, and not because of his height. Tensely aloof, he held himself as though listening out for an alert, perhaps a sniper ready to shoot from a neighbouring rooftop, his narrow, bony head with its huge beak of a nose cocked slightly to one side, like a big bird, she thought, a stork perhaps, ready to go into ungainly flight.

Edith withdrew from the window, fearful that he might see her spying on him.

During the following days she would hear him, on occasion, struggling up with his weight of water, and shyly, discreetly, stay on her floor until she heard him go indoors before descending. But once she did run into him, unexpectedly, and his immense eyes, protruding, made a flicking, swivelling motion, to avoid her. They passed each other without a word, except for a faint gesture of acknowledgement.

· 5 ·

Edith heard the telephone ringing through an unending dream in which she was attempting to carry her mother up the stairs. It was the middle of the night, a cold wind was blowing from open windows, and both she and her mother were clad only in thin cotton shifts. The body of her mother was a dead weight, and her muscles ached with the strain. Arms tight round her neck, Mrs Johnson had her head turned to the stars in the night sky beyond the window, and was reciting their names out loud. Astonishingly, she could identify each and every one of them, even the smallest, the most remote, and sang out a jumble of alien words which made no sense to Edith, who was getting angry, not just at the weight bearing down on her, but at the old woman's superior knowledge, from which she was shut out.

She was glad when the sound of the telephone interrupted the flow of incomprehensible words, and she found herself in bed, with daylight visible through a gap in the curtains. Yawning, stretching aching limbs, Edith lifted the receiver.

It was Rhoda, her voice booming cheerfully down the line. I'm back, she bellowed. Then, sensing uncertainty, she added: Sorry, did I wake you?

Edith sat up, hurriedly trying to collect the bits of herself, and fit them together. Rhoda was always so strong, so hearty, she went at everything with a will. Sometimes this imbued Edith with a sense of her own feebleness, as it did now. She hastily denied that she had been still asleep.

How was it? she demanded, knowing that Rhoda was going to tell her anyhow.

Edith settled herself more comfortably in bed as Rhoda embarked on a full account of her walking holiday, leaving almost nothing out. The weather had been changeable, cloud and light rain alternating with brief sunny spells, but it was not too bad. Now and then it was slippery underfoot, but the rain was not too heavy for the most part. The terrain had been tricky, even challenging on occasion, but the group had covered the ground according to plan, with only minor injuries. She herself had got off lightly, with a few blisters and a badly strained shoulder, brought on by her backpack, though one member of the group had injured an ankle. Edith listened to a description of rocks, uplands, fording mountain streams, wild countryside without a soul to be seen, stretches of purple heather, and felt weariness overcoming her. She sagged into her pillows. If she had not been a neighbour, and a good sort, Edith would never have sought the company of a woman who taught physical education, her worst subject when she was at school. And Rhoda lived up to the principles she taught, fully, up to the hilt. Age had not dimmed her enthusiasm, her youthful optimism. But the thought of bending and stretching, let alone of conquering wild terrain for the sake of it, sapped Edith's wilting spirit.

Rhoda, having disposed of the uplands, ended her brisk verbal tour by coming back to earth. 'Mother well?' she enquired lightly, clearly not expecting to hear anything to the contrary. Edith told her, knowing from the uneasy mutterings, the muffled expletives coming through the receiver, that her friend was, for the moment, at a loss, nonplussed by the truth. Edith took the opportunity to be frank.

Rhoda had been friendly with old Mrs Johnson, in a hearty sort of way. She used to call in regularly, rather casually, never staying for long. In the past few years, as her mobility was reduced, first to the second floor, then to the living room for a few hours each day, and at last to the chair beside her bed, Rhoda Simpson cheerfully continued to regard the old lady as in the peak of condition. All symptoms were merely passing inconveniences, to be endured lightly, with cheerful stoicism. I know you're as fit as a fiddle, she would say in her brusque, jolly voice, popping her head round the door of Mrs Johnson's bedroom, and withdrawing it promptly, pre-empting the opportunity to deny it.

There was a longish silence after Edith finished speaking. She could hear Rhoda breathing heavily.

I expect it's for the best.

Her words, when they came, lacked their usual sense of conviction, but Rhoda was trying hard.

*

Later that day, when the sky had grown dark beyond the rooftops, water suddenly began spluttering through the pipes. It was a hard, rasping sound and, coming unexpectedly, startled Edith out of her end-of-the-day drowsiness. From kitchen and bathroom she heard a hollow wheezing and coughing, a spluttering and gasping, which sent her hurrying into the kitchen just as the first weak spurt of water issued from the cold tap.

After only a few seconds more air came gasping out, but it was a beginning. A resumption of normality was also signalled by other sounds, a juddering and jarring of the old lead pipes, a sclerotic gurgling in the archaic water heater and, in the roof space overhead, the hollow sound of the ancient tank beginning to fill. Edith knew it would be many hours before there was sufficient pressure for hot water, so no bath tonight. But the prospect of having one in the morning was by now enough to send her happily to bed, after a perfunctory wash. Fragments of rust and grit spattered into the basin, and the water was as yet far from clean. Edith had known for years that the tank was only held together by rust, a plumber had told her so, and for years she had been expecting it to pour its contents through her ceiling, no doubt bringing it crashing down. But for now she was too content at the restoration of the water supply to return to this perpetual, nagging worry. And physical fatigue sent her into a profound and dreamless sleep.

She woke to joyous birdsong, and drew back her curtains to let in a flood of sunlight, showing up dust on her dark wardrobe. In the kitchen she filled the kettle, heard the water still spluttering a bit.

But when she settled down to her first cup of the day,

43

Edith found the tea tasted distinctly peculiar, and also had an unpleasant odour. She took several sips to make sure she was not imagining this, then filled a glass under the cold tap. It smelt bad, and tasted worse. Edith held the glass up to the light. Its contents were murky and glaucous, and she could see little bits floating about. When she took the glass to the window it became obvious that the bits were not floating, but swimming. Myriads of tiny grubs, vigorously thrashing about.

Feeling sick, Edith spat, spat, spat, then washed her mouth out with mineral water. She felt nauseous enough to try retching, but brought nothing up. She reminded herself that the water had been boiled, no grubs could be swimming inside her, it only felt as if they were.

Edith hurriedly got dressed and went down to visit Rhoda. Getting no reply, she rang the bell again, listening to the stillness after the sound ceased. Waiting impatiently, she thought of trying to disturb the Wolfs, thought better of it, heard nothing from Rhoda's rooms, and banged on the door, calling out her name. Eventually she could hear slow footsteps, the floorboards creaking, and the door was drawn slightly ajar. Rhoda peered out, looking dishevelled and uncharacteristically vague, as though she did not know Edith. It took her a moment, seemingly, to recognise her. Slowly, fumbling a bit, she took off the safety chain and let her in.

Rhoda was still in a dressing gown, her hair unkempt, her skin an ashen colour. Dark shadows under her eyes. To Edith she seemed shockingly ill.

I feel awful, Rhoda croaked huskily, going through to the living room. Been up half the night, sick as a dog. Must be something I ate.

44

Drank, retorted Edith firmly. It's the water. There's something wrong with it. I just found out.

Rhoda did not have a proper hall, only a long passage with doors on either side. This morning they all stood open, shedding dusty light on the rumpled carpet riding up from the creaking floorboards. A bulging rucksack had been propped up against the wall, and Edith had to edge her way past it.

The living room was tiny, the furniture too big for it. Rhoda had sunk into an armchair, heavy and inert as a sack of potatoes. She let her head loll back, eyes shut.

You think so? You worry too much, that's your problem.

She opened one eye to look mockingly at Edith and immediately shut it again.

That's why I came down, to warn you. Perhaps I should tell everybody. Though how anyone could fail to notice it is beyond me. Didn't you taste it, and smell it? And if you hold it up to the light—

Looking at Rhoda's inert form, her livid colour, Edith decided not to go on. Even Rhoda, who was not finicky about food, might find it too much just now. Edith knew her liking for strong, cheap, instant coffee, and suspected that this might have disguised the dreadful odour and flavour, given that Rhoda's taste buds were not too particular. She regarded food simply as a necessary fuel, and eating as a tedious function to be got through with a minimum of fuss.

Rhoda suddenly clutched both hands to her lower abdomen and emitted a groan. Her broad face with its heavy jowl was twisted in a grimace.

And Felix has vanished.

Rhoda made an effort to sit up and looked Edith straight in the eyes.

Surely not?

Rhoda was staring at her in a faintly accusing manner, and Edith tried to appear both innocent, which she was, and duly concerned, which, deep down, she was not.

Chris has been coming up to feed him, but there's no sign of him now.

I expect he'll turn up.

Edith was conscious of her own hypocrisy. The most she could feel for cats was a respectful coolness, but she found it impossible to harbour any such sentiment for Felix, who looked like a torn old rag, with a similar stink to him. He was disgusting, and it would gladden her heart to see the last of him. She was fed up with finding his hairs on her skirt, clawmarks on the bannister, a strong odour on landings, and murdered booty lying on the front steps. It made her both angry and sad to find those pathetic bundles of feathers with their tiny beaks, knowing they had been bereft of flight and joy for the hell of it, and that the old tom was boasting of his victory. It was surprising to her, and also a bit galling, that Rhoda should have got away with keeping him for so long, it being contrary to the landlord's rules to keep pets. But the landlord rarely visited, and when he did so he was more concerned with the actual building, the condition of the structure, than with anything that might occur within it. And if none of the tenants had thought fit to complain, no doubt they had their reasons. Edith herself could do nothing, obviously, on account of her friendship with Rhoda, even though the animal could stretch loyalty to the limit. The Wolfs were much too timid to risk alienating anybody, and Jane Lamb was not only too kind to report anybody behind their back, but had a dog – Chris's pet – in her flat. No, Mrs Gardiner was the obvious person to do it. She did not get on with Rhoda, was a stickler for landlord's rules, and was forever complaining about Felix's disgusting habits. Edith could only think that Mrs Gardiner had her own reasons for saying nothing, or that she had perhaps reported the matter to the landlord without success.

I expect he'll turn up, she heard herself repeating, and almost hoped he would, upset by Rhoda's sickly pallor, her uncharacteristic passivity. Felix must have nine lives.

She said it cheerfully, having thought as much herself, gloomily, when she heard him howling through so many restless nights, eerie as a banshee beyond the window. This ugly animal was a far cry from the leaping, licking, tail-wagging puppy a doting but misguided uncle had given young Chris a few years back. His worried mother, unable to withstand her son's joy, had spent time winning round the neighbours. Who could resist her, or her fatherless child? Besides, the darling little puppy had grown up into a mild, silken-haired spaniel, quiet, forever friendly, licking fingers, wagging his tail. Just as Chris had grown up with good looks and good manners, ever polite and helpful. But Rhoda was brusque, and not particularly lovable.

I think you should call a doctor.

Edith got up. She felt it her duty to warn the other tenants.

Doctors, mumbled Rhoda. Don't believe in them. Never had a day's illness in my life.

Well, you have now, Edith said shortly, and left.

She banged loudly on the Wolfs' door, urgency giving

47

her confidence. But she heard nothing, no footsteps on creaking floorboards, no sound of inner doors moving. A disturbing vision of the two of them still asleep, no, not sleeping, profoundly unconscious, came uninvited into her head and, though she attempted to dismiss it, would keep lingering. It was not just that they were old, an aura of uncommon fragility clung to them. Hearing nothing, Edith went back upstairs to scrawl a note, which she slipped under their front door. TAP WATER POISONOUS she wrote in large capitals, adding, DON'T DRINK. After she had pushed it through she paused a moment, listening. She thought she heard breathing, though whether it was merely a draught, the wind blowing under a door, or her own body, she could not be sure. A low subdued cough, undoubtedly the sound of somebody stirring, sent sudden relief surging through her, and she hurried down to the main door, knowing her note would be found, not wishing to be seen.

Jane came to the door of the basement flat moments after she had rung the bell.

I know about the water, she told Edith. You only have to smell it. But Chris is sick. He gulped it down in a hurry last night. He'd been running, and just drank without thinking. I've been up half the night.

Her face was anxious, pallid with lack of sleep. Edith followed her indoors.

I don't like the look of him, even though he's not vomiting now. He still has abdominal pains, and feels feverish.

Is there anything I can do?

Edith had been helping out ever since Chris was a very small child, but now he was long past wanting her to sit by

48

his bed, reading outlandish fairy tales, touching him, holding him, giving him a drink, if Jane had to go out. Nevertheless, there were other ways of doing what she could.

Not a lot. Though I'd be glad of some more mineral water, if you are going out to the shops. I've already sent for the doctor, and no doubt he'll get an analysis, to confirm it is the water. You might warn the neighbours.

Jane stood in the shadows, looking haggard, limp strands of lacklustre fair hair hanging round her thin face. He fell asleep about an hour ago, she added, keeping her voice down, as the two women stood on her front step. The sun would not reach the lower depths of her concrete area for hours, though sky and rooftops were bright.

She found Mrs Gardiner in the hallway, snooping through her post, as she always did, given the opportunity. Clearly she had not been affected by the noxious water, either because she had not drunk it, or because her constitution was tough enough to withstand its effects. She turned her meticulously kempt head as Edith entered the main door, and did not so much as flinch at being caught red-handed. Her face was lightly powdered, she wore pearl button earrings and an ivory satin blouse with a big bow. Oh no, she had not touched the stuff, one sniff was enough to warn her, besides, not a drop of tap water had passed her lips in years. Though her cleaning woman had been foolish enough to drink it, had just rung to say she was too sick to come this morning. Which was exceedingly annoying, since she had a visitor coming this afternoon.

Angrily, Edith snatched the letters from Mrs Gardiner's ringed and freckled fingers. She did it with sufficient emphasis to make it clear that a misdemeanour had occurred, though in the event only two letters were addressed to her. Not even letters: a bank statement and a picture postcard. But the bank statement had been partly prised open, and no doubt she had also studied the coloured photograph and read the cryptic, impersonal message on the other side. There were several bills for Mrs Gardiner, which she handed back. Mrs Gardiner told her that she had become very long-sighted, so it was difficult for her to read inscriptions, and Edith suggested tartly that she let other people sort out the post, thus solving the problem. And went abruptly up the staircase.

By late afternoon the water lorry was once more parked outside, bringing fresh water from another district, and now a system of rationing was imposed. Edith had been shopping, but found that the supermarket was limiting the number of bottles it sold to each customer, whilst the corner shop had run out of mineral water altogether.

By the time Edith brought a few bottles of water to the basement, the doctor had been and gone. Apparently half the neighbourhood was sick, and there had been outbreaks in other parts of the city. Prognosis was difficult, since the pathogen was as yet unknown. The symptoms might last hours, or days, might or might not have long-term consequences, he could not say, no doubt depending on individual constitutions. He heard about Rhoda Simpson whilst examining the boy but, since she was not on his list and he had not been sent for, did not go up to the first floor. He had, he said, a dozen patients still to see, all with similar symptoms.

.6.

Normal water supply was not restored for weeks. On several occasions during that period the taps spluttered and spurted for an hour or so, then dried up. Once the water came through a deep rust colour, another time it was bluish and smelt of bad eggs. Leaflets were pushed through the door, and an official from the water authority called on each household, wearing a dark suit and uttering assurances which soothed nobody. Edith found herself feeling slightly sorry for him, knowing that he must face constant hostility, even though killing the messenger is futile. By this time people in the neighbourhood were so angry, so utterly fed up, that the promise of an eventual refund did nothing to mollify them.

Rhoda was still unwell, but could not be persuaded to send for the doctor. She spent most of the time lying in bed, but occasionally moved to an armchair in her untidy living room, wrapped in a discoloured old bathrobe, her feet in downtrodden slippers, grey hair tousled and unkempt. Edith fetched water from the street, and brought in bottled water. But she felt unable to do much more in the face of Rhoda's lassitude, her apparent unwillingness to help herself by calling a doctor. She would fuss around now and then, but the flat was in a mess. Unwashed clothes were strewn in the bedroom, where Rhoda would not let her change the sheets. Dirty crockery kept piling up in the kitchen, whilst a thick film of dust covered the living-room furniture. And the backpack still stood near the front door, left there since the night of Rhoda's return, bulging.

Edith had never seen Rhoda Simpson so listless, so utterly indifferent to her surroundings. She did not even mention Felix now, as if his continuing absence no longer concerned her. It disturbed her to see this great ox of a woman, with her booming voice and aggressive energy, suddenly so changed. She had lost weight, but her slack skin looked far from healthy, and her complexion was yellowish. If she had been less stressed herself she might have tried chivvying her into action, but surviving from day to day was now very hard, and it was as much as she could do to get through the day. Dragging heavy weights of water up the stairs was exhausting, especially in the increasingly hot weather. Each trip seemed to defeat its own end, resulting in thirst, sweating, and a deep longing for a refreshing bath.

Chris Lamb, on the other hand, was soon well enough to go back to school, having made a quick recovery, and this helped to lift Edith's spirits. He would sometimes help her out at weekends, carrying water up, and the sight of him, skin turning brown, fair hair bleached paler by the hour until it was eye-catching in its purity, would always cheer her up.

*

The hot weather continued. The grass in the Lambs' back garden turned brown, the sounds and smells of the road drifted through open windows during the day. At night music and loud voices could be heard through the silent trees. Their leaves hung limp, asphalt in the road grew sticky, and all sense of seclusion was dispersed in the stifling air.

Early on a Thursday morning Edith, on her way downstairs, found a huge crack running down the length of the wall beyond her front door. It ran from the high ceiling to the skirting board on her landing, near the corner, as though the house frontage was coming away from the side. Bits of plaster were crumbling out of the fissure, which was wide enough for her to push her fingers halfway in.

Edith sat down suddenly on the steps, feeling her legs turn weak with shock. Her reaction was of numb disbelief and, underneath it, a dawning recognition that she had been blind to the obvious. The building had stood for so long and, although joists creaked and the plumbing was severely defective, the structure had always appeared sound, solid as a rock. So it was possible to disregard the fact that the house was old, that not much cash had been spent on it, and that old buildings eventually hit the dust. Now the moment had come, for her, when its solidity was in doubt. Edith's reasoning mind told her that the house was subsiding, the result of a long spell of dry weather, of several periods of drought. This conclusion was alarming.

She got up from the step on which she had been sitting, looking at the fissure rising above her head, and walked down to the floor below. Her legs still felt shaky, but she was greatly relieved to find that the crack did not continue

53

this far, not yet, anyhow. Downstairs she found Mrs Gardiner prying through a handful of letters, but for once Edith was not angry at the sight, and did not attempt to snatch them from her. She told her, rather urgently, what she had just seen on the second floor.

Come up and see for yourself.

Edith could not recall when Mrs Gardiner had last climbed to the second floor, but this was an emergency. To her astonishment her neighbour handed over her post, only bills, and walked off.

Nothing to do with me, she retorted firmly, before vanishing through her front door. Edith heard her turning the second lock, then putting up the safety chain.

She had thought, in the spring, that her life would be enriched by new opportunity, now that the constant responsibility for mother had been taken from her. But so far minor daydreams had had to be postponed indefinitely. She had not got round to buying flowers, nor found a piano tuner. Visiting had to be put off, and coping with difficulty took all her time and energy. By the end of the day she felt utterly exhausted. And if she no longer had to drag water upstairs, she was still trying to catch up on a backlog of domestic chores which had simply been left during the emergency.

Now there was a fresh emergency to occupy her mind. The alarming crack in the outer wall took priority, pushing all other concerns into the background. Edith decided to send a letter to the landlord.

This task took all day, as she knew it would. Writing to the landlord was not an undertaking to be lightly entered into, and she thought long and hard before embarking on what was merely a first draft. She felt it was important to press upon him the urgency of the situation, but without sounding too alarmist. To do so was to risk a charge of hysteria, of disproportionate fussing, which could be ignored. And she had heard stories of landlords who found major building work the ideal excuse for getting rid of tenants. She did not think he would do such a thing, or that the work required could warrant it, nevertheless nobody could afford to be other than extremely careful in committing pen to paper. Such a letter, if badly phrased, might ultimately be used against her. It might be argued, for instance, that she had herself forced the landlord to embark on a course of action, without due regard to the consequences; if she was the unwitting victim, she had brought it on herself. In all her dealings with the landlord, Edith trod an uneasy tightrope. She was constantly wary, fearful of unforeseen consequences, of breaking the letter or spirit of the law. On the other hand she had rights, which she had no intention of forgoing. She had always thought it a citizen's duty to exert such rights with vigour, if only for the sake of the community, for the future. Too much timidity was tantamount to choosing to be the victim, thus giving licence to rapacity, to the unscrupulous.

The landlord visited the house without warning the following week. He was a small, mild-mannered man who had come into the business, not by planning and acquisition, but as a result of his father's death a few years back. He was much more informal than his father, who had been a stickler for breaches of tenancy agreements, and employed an agent to inspect the premises at regular intervals to ensure that nobody was behaving unlawfully, hanging out washing, sub-letting or failing to clean the windows. His son, on the other hand, did not answer correspondence, sent out shoddy rent demands, and seldom put in an appearance. The agent had long since vanished and, if the upkeep of the house was now slightly neglected, the tenants had come to the conclusion that he did not much mind what they did, as long as the rent was paid promptly. Rhoda would never have had the temerity to acquire a smelly old tomcat like Felix when his father was still living.

Nothing to be done about it, the landlord told Edith, looking up at the long crack, his head thrown back. He banged the wall on either side of the fissure with a balled fist. The building is subsiding. Too many hot summers, not enough rain. The whole city is built on clay.

He poked his fingers into the crack. He had small, neat hands, the left with a plain gold wedding ring. In spite of the hot weather he was wearing a formal grey suit. Now he rubbed the dust off his fingers, shook his head. His greying hair, like his fingernails, had been trimmed short, tidily.

Nothing I can do. This is not bad, not really. I've seen far worse recently, believe me.

To Edith his voice sounded resigned, impossibly complacent.

Why don't you do something now, to prevent it getting worse?

She felt emboldened to speak out. But the landlord shook his head, regretfully, almost kindly.

This building is getting towards the end of its useful life. The costs would be out of all proportion to returns.

I'll look into the question of insurance, but I doubt whether they will pay up. Not if they can find a way out. Though the premiums are going up at an appalling rate on account of the drought, they still don't like paying for it. And then, you risk doing more harm than good with this kind of structure. For a start, I would have to move the tenants in the basement, and I doubt whether they would go willingly, so that might mean legal costs. I'll look into it but, as I say, it's hardly worth the upheaval. The condition might not get worse for ages, old houses have a tendency simply to settle down, to shift their ground slightly. All part of growing old.

He laughed gently, looking at her for a moment, inviting her understanding, complicity, but Edith was trying to control tumultuous surges of panic. She did not know which thought was more dreadful, driving out the Lambs, whom she loved, or the front of the house falling away, a nightmare vision which had been haunting her for the past week.

Once here, the landlord took the opportunity to inspect the rest of the house. He began with Edith's flat, moving casually from room to room, glancing at grey ceilings, looking, so Edith felt, disparagingly at the wisps of cobweb floating in corners and the rather dismal state of her walls. She mumbled something about leaking taps, the sclerotic plumbing in the bathroom. He simply made casual remarks about fitting new washers and treating the outflow with chemicals. In her mother's vacant bedroom she told him of her difficulty with the sash windows, which did not fit properly in any of the rooms. Either she could not get them open, or they would not shut. And they were terribly draughty in winter. Had she thought of fitting draught excluders? he asked, pulling at a badly frayed sashcord. They were very cheap, and she could easily fit them herself. And she should try rubbing a candle along the frames to stop them from getting stuck. The landlord had now found a window quite devoid of sashcords: Edith had given up on it years ago, and kept it permanently shut. He gave her a reproachful look, and Edith felt uneasy. She had been told that even sashcords and tap washers were the landlord's responsibility, but she did not have the temerity to tell him.

Looking at her dreary walls, the landlord went on to remark that the rooms were in need of redecoration. He said it coolly, without obvious reproach. Edith felt herself blushing, and her heart thrashing like a trapped bird. Yes, she admitted, but she had been caring for her elderly mother until recently, making it totally impracticable.

And so the landlord took his leave, civilly enough, with Edith feeling as though he had unexpectedly become the complainant. Edith was not quite sure how this had come about, except that her own timidity, her own uncertainty, had somehow swung the balance in his favour. And then she could not help seeing the situation from his point of view. She knew that if she were in his position she would be resentful of the tenants here, would be constantly prevaricating, finding excuses. The profits were neg- ligible, the problems without end.

She heard him on the floor below, trying unsuccessfully to rouse Rhoda, exchanging words with Martha Wolf. Edith was cross with herself for not pressing him; she went over their conversation, trying to pinpoint where she had let him gain the upper hand. She was fearful of him, this was the truth. Though mild enough, she knew he was a hungry dog on a leash, and it was only the law which held him back, not his intrinsic nature. And so she found no way of engaging with him, not really.

She was living on shifting ground now, with a deeper, if underlying anxiety which was new, so that most of her normal preoccupations suddenly seemed myopic, a bit silly.

· 7 ·

Edith had begun to get rid of several items of furniture brought to the flat by her mother. The wing-backed armchair, now dismally shabby, was the first to go. One fine Saturday morning Chris helped to carry it down the staircase, grasping the two front feet whilst Edith held on to the head, and so, with unceremonious bumping and sliding, they got it down to street level and left it near the dustbins.

And there it stayed. After a few days Edith rang up the council, feeling inexplicably guilty at the continuing sight of it. Rubbish collection had become infrequent and unreliable during the past months, and by now the dustmen would not pick up bulky items without prior notice. She was told there would be a delay of several weeks before it could be taken away. She could, on the other hand, drive it to the nearest dump. Edith left her address and hung up.

It disturbed her slightly to see it, day in, day out, slowly getting more dilapidated. A torn lampshade and several tin cans now lay on the seat, and the upholstery was dark with weather, like a vagrant's clothing. Mrs Gardiner had begun to complain that it was unsightly. She saw a cat digging its claws into the cloth, prowling round it. Edith saw her mother sitting in the chair, rubbish in her lap, a sparrow pecking at her grey hair, and felt bad about it continuing to stand by the dustbins.

Not that she had any qualms about rearranging her rooms. On the contrary, she felt she should do so, that her wellbeing, perhaps her sanity, depended upon it. But the armchair, standing as it now did, a forlorn bit of rubbish, was too accusing for comfort. It kept getting dirtier, had lost its colour, and began to stink. So she felt she could not throw out any more of Mrs Johnson's bits and pieces for the time being. Not as long as the armchair still stood in the alley, grey stuffing spilling out of it. By now its condition was too dreadful to tempt even scavengers.

And the collection of ordinary rubbish seemed to have ceased indefinitely. The bins were long since full, now bulging plastic bags were put on them, round them, into and around the armchair, in what was becoming a growing mountain. Cardboard boxes lay nearby, full of old newspapers. At night marauding cats and dogs, no doubt the odd city fox too, split the thin plastic wrapping to spill vegetable peelings and leftover bones. Rotting scraps of food began to stink in the hot weather. Even from her floor Edith could smell it during the day.

Mrs Gardiner was loud in her complaints, but did nothing. The smell was dreadful, she did not know what to do, blaming the greedy dustmen, was it any wonder law-abiding people were refusing to pay out ever higher taxes. The Lambs, on the other hand, who were just as badly affected, made a conscious effort to limit the filth, and took to sweeping up the area round the dustbins each evening. The swish of a broom could be heard through the open windows during the slow sultry dusk.

With the situation continuing indefinitely, Chris organised a bonfire in the back garden.

The bonfire night was fun. Born out of necessity, it nevertheless acquired the aura of a celebratory ritual. All week, after he got back from school, Chris had been constructing a monumental pyre, consisting of anything that would burn easily, and was expendable. Cardboard, old shelving, newspapers, bit by bit he assembled the detritus of living so it would hold together for the moment. Items of old clothing were stuffed into interstices, together with bits of soft furnishing now rotting to shreds. And Mrs Johnson's chair sat perched on top, a mock martyr, or travesty of state.

Chris finally put a match to the pyre on Saturday evening, and several of the neighbours had come round to watch. Small children, allowed to stay up unusually late because of the hot weather, ran round the garden, screeching excitedly. When the flames took hold, hissing, setting off minor explosions, adults held them back from going too near. Bright sparks showered upward, grey ash descended slowly. It fell on shoulders, caught in thick hair. But pleasurable excitement turned to terror when a nearby tree was set alight, beginning to burn with unexpected ferocity. Children were hastily marshalled, buckets of water fetched, the flames doused, leaving a mess of black, steaming cinders, also the charred skeleton of Mrs Johnson's armchair.

*

There were rumours of rats seen in the neighbourhood. Edith slept badly during the hot nights, saw her mother being burnt in effigy on the back lawn, and put a bunch of yellow tulips near the charred cinders. She kept her windows open, but by now the whiff of rotten garbage blew in even at night. Martha Wolf had brought up a box of incense sticks, and she took to burning them in the evening, before she went to bed. But the curious, rather sickly odour was at first overwhelming, then ineffective.

Jane Lamb was the only tenant who had a car, and she made several trips to the rubbish dump. Others in the neighbourhood, being less scrupulous, simply left refuse anywhere, so long as it was far from their own doorstep, often after dark. A residential square nearby rapidly turned into a dumping ground, as did the street corner with its grand old drinking fountain under a spreading chestnut tree. It was not uncommon to find the Lambs' attempts at order undone in the night, not by marauding animals, but unneighbourly neighbours.

A kind of stasis seemed to hang over the world. Edith was still thinking of buying flowers, though not tulips, for Mrs Johnson, but had not got round to it. As for the piano, and getting it tuned, she did not even think about it now. It was as much as she could do to get through the day. The atmosphere was suffocating, with no breath of refreshing wind. Trees, now in full leaf, hung dusty and limp.

Rhoda Simpson was still sick, and the sight of her made Edith uneasy. She was losing far too much weight, and her grey skin almost hung off her. But Edith, herself unable to eat much in this hot weather, had neither sufficient conviction nor energy to coax food into her. Besides, she was beginning to think there was more to Rhoda's illness than water poisoning. No doubt people were affected with varying degrees of severity, but she should have got over it by now. No, there was something distinctly odd about her refusal to see a doctor, to submit to the most elementary tests. An underlying lethargy had transformed her into a being Edith scarcely recognised. This was not the Rhoda who boasted of never even catching a cold, who had not taken a day's sick leave in twenty years. Once or twice she took down a jug of delicious lemonade, and sat with her whilst she drank it, but it was dispiriting, now that Rhoda was so taciturn. Edith knew she should nag her to consult a doctor, but was fearful of irritating her. Rhoda had also become grumpy.

When the weather got cooler, Edith told herself, she would try to find a piano tuner. Just now her fingers felt like swollen sausages anyhow. The journey was far too trying in this heat, but when it broke she would go out to the suburbs with a flowering pot plant. Mrs Johnson had always liked azaleas, pink particularly. And she would search her little attic room for the painting materials she had kept up there, though the tubes of colour might be far too dry by now. Still, she could buy new ones, once she had the energy to make plans, get going. And perhaps she should first of all try to make the rooms a bit more cheerful, rather more a reflection of her own soul. That was what she had wanted, when she first moved in. She had visualised white walls and pretty colours, a space in which light fell like harmony, but contingencies had always intervened. Not that she had such high ideals now, on the contrary. But the landlord was justified in saying the rooms were neglected. As soon as the weather got cooler she would look at her savings account, and perhaps get one or two estimates.

Meanwhile she took to lying on her bed during the hottest hours of the day, dozing or daydreaming, looking up at the familiar stains and floating cobwebs of the high old ceiling. She thought about what to do with the room that had been her mother's, but came to no firm conclusion. She would like to grow plants, or use it as a studio. Then again, perhaps this was just fanciful. She found herself listening for any sounds from below, from the Wolfs' rooms. Martha smiled at her now, and exchanged a few words, though she had not come upstairs recently. Her brother continued to stay aloof, though he had been briefly visible during the conflagration in the back garden. Edith had seen him standing at a first-floor window behind reflecting flames, then vanish. Fragments of poetry memorized in the schoolroom drifted in and out of her mind. She heard a plane droning off in the distance, and slept for an hour.

The hot spell ended suddenly, with a thunderstorm. Light rapidly grew dim, a distant rumble in gathering clouds, and rain was falling steadily, sheeting down. It was a relief to feel the atmosphere cool with every passing moment, smell the fresh odour which only a downpour, long withheld, can bring. There was an aura of benediction about it, the trees totally immersed, leaves washing clean. The dry earth grew dark, drinking it in. Edith saw bedraggled dogs running, tails flashing, and the road suddenly a swollen river, its gutters overwhelmed. Uncollected rubbish was running downstream, choking in drains, building up dams with water eddying round it. At the back of the house the Lambs' lawn was now a marsh, the flower borders waterlogged. Edith found it exhilarating, the sound and smell of it, after the long hot weeks of drought. That is, until she heard the sound of water dripping indoors.

. 8 .

Water was dripping through her bedroom ceiling. The room which her mother once occupied had also sprung a leak. Edith hurriedly put out large pans to catch the drops, and the sound of water hitting metal soon modulated to a softer, splashing rhythm as the vessels filled. She went from room to room, seeking further signs of water penetration. Living room, kitchen and bathroom showed nothing as yet. But the little attic room was in a dreadful mess. It was reached by a narrow winding stair which Mrs Johnson, even during her fit period, found too treacherous to climb, and Edith had used the room mainly to store the kind of personal memorabilia which her mother would have found irresistible, and which Edith would rather Mrs Johnson did not see. But she herself rarely went up there.

Now water was running down the sloping attic roof and into the bureau which stood beneath it. Her first thought was to try to shift the bureau away from the wall, to the middle of the floor, but it was far too heavy. And she knew she had to be wary of putting undue strain on her back: a weak muscle near her left hip could go so easily if she attempted to lift anything heavy, and once it went she would be helpless for days afterwards. So she took out the lower drawers first, spilling their dusty contents on the floor. Too much stuff, the drawers jammed before she could pull them free. Bundles of old letters on crumbling discoloured paper, torn envelopes and discontinued postage stamps, photographs, ancient theatre programmes, forgotten postcards of unremembered resorts, or not remembered like this, the dry detritus of anguish and joy. She had consciously chosen not to look at this stuff for years now, even though she had kept it, even though she could not bring herself to throw it out. She knew that one day she must get rid of it, leave nothing behind. But now she had it out, the entire dusty mess, she carefully put the stuff back, smoothing, sorting, reading signatures.

She had been a fool, no doubt about it. Mrs Johnson had said so, constantly, and Edith conceded the point. And yet, moment by moment, she could not have been different, nor would she have wished it. She found a funny postcard from Derek, who had once occupied this room for five months, paying her no rent, though lots of attention. Not that she had been particularly hurt, well, not dreadfully, she had let him occupy the room from kindness, mostly, since she had it, did not need it herself, and what occurred between them had been fortuitous, perhaps almost incidental, the result of proximity. Nevertheless she had not expected such fecklessness, such deceit. What had really hurt her, when he went off without so much as a word, packing his things and going whilst she was out at work, was his theft of the opal ring. Theft was theft, and the ring meant a lot to her. It was the only valuable thing Clive had ever given her, well, he had a family to support, and buying jewellery was too much of a commitment. She understood this, did not hold it against him, but now she had so little to remember him by. She could not suppress a sneaking suspicion that he had been fearful of blackmail, and this was why he so seldom committed himself to paper, except for that last letter, which she had torn up instantly, in a fury of wild emotion such as she would rather not recall. Even now it hurt her to think of it, and then, still very shaken by the abortion, upset not just by the physical stress but by the heartbreaking loss (she had so wanted his child, their child, dreaming of a small boy with his features), it had been too much for her.

Clearly the leaks in the roof justified calling the landlord right away, but her telephone was not functioning. Edith spent the best part of an hour trying to get a connection. Each attempt increased her feeling of helplessness. Getting frantic, she went down to ring Rhoda's doorbell, but got no reply. There was no sound from behind the Wolfs' door, and no light visible through the glass above it. Edith stood for a moment, daring herself to thump on the door, her heart beating faster at the thought of doing so. Earlier on she had heard the brother creeping about. Perhaps he was on his own. It was the possibility of having to speak to him, rather than Martha, that deterred her from going through with it now.

She went back to the second floor in a mood of

indecision. The rain had eased off, and with it the persistent drip drip. Perhaps things would get back to normal, she thought, seeing a refuse truck unexpectedly working its way down the road. Dustmen went to and fro, lifting several bags in each gloved hand, tossing rubbish into the back of the truck, emptying bins into its grinding mouth. The massive vehicle continued slowly along the street, leaving behind a wake of litter on the freshly rinsed pavement, or running in waterlogged gutters.

Edith heard the buzzer with annoyance, knowing it was likely to be a nuisance, either a religious nut who had found God and was eager to share the good news, a foreigner seeking an unknown person, or a frustrated driver trying to find the owner of a car blocking his own. Often it was difficult to comprehend the human voice through the entry system, prolonging the silly exchange unnecessarily.

But the voice now coming through was distinct, and very assured. A man's voice, saying he was looking for Edith Johnson, daughter of Muriel Johnson. Nothing dubious about it, on the contrary, it sounded too officious for comfort. Edith felt panic-stricken, not knowing what to expect, fearing the worst.

The visitor took his time, getting to her landing. Edith could hear him lumbering slowly upward, breathing heavily, taking frequent rests, saw a plump hand on the bannister. She caught a glimpse of a bulky figure, heard wheezing lungs. When he finally reached the second floor this immense creature, fat bulging out of his suit, several chins spilling over his tight collar, was panting for breath. Beads of sweat stood out on his large forehead.

Seeing him so flustered by the climb, Edith did not first

ask after either his identity or his mission before letting him in. She led him into the living room, indicating a chair which could scarcely accommodate him. She even offered to fetch a glass of water, but he shook his head, dabbing the sweat on his swarthy skin with a checkered handkerchief. Fumbling for an identity card, the man held it under her eyes.

You shouldn't admit strangers, he said, still fighting for breath.

Edith understood the danger, but also knew that she had to admit him. Knowing her mother's first name, and hers, this gave him some kind of authority, obviously. Instinct told her his visit was not auspicious, but she had to confront him.

His mission, however, when he found sufficient breath to tell her, was so far from anything she might have feared, so totally absurd, that she simply burst out laughing. He had come, he informed her, in his official capacity, on behalf of an old man, now extremely infirm and consequently a burden on the taxpayer, who had recently expressed an unexpected but fervent wish to re-establish relations with his family, namely his wife Muriel, also their mutual offspring.

Her mirth subsiding, Edith told him there had clearly been a clerical error. He had come to the wrong address, to the wrong Johnson: her father, of whom she had almost no memory, had not survived the war. Missing in action, presumed killed. He was a hero, flying over enemy territory. All she had of him now was a photograph, a young man in uniform.

She went to fetch it, placing the familiar icon between his plump fingers, which, like his nostrils, had short black hairs growing from them.

My father, she said. They shall not grow old, as we that are left grow old. Such a good-looking young man, don't you think? She spoke fondly, proudly. My poor mother never stopped hoping, not for a moment, not until the war was well and truly over, the last prisoner back with his family. There was always a chance, she said, trying to keep our spirits up. He might have come down somewhere, to spend the rest of the war in hiding. She did not want us to think we had no father, to put him behind us, as children will. And no doubt she was trying to keep her own spirits up, but in the end she had to accept it.

Her visitor looked uneasy, fiddling with the framed photograph, putting it down.

Your parents were divorced shortly after the war. My department has had sight of the relevant documents, both nisi and absolute.

Edith felt her legs giving way under her. The visitor was sitting slackly in his chair, but it was as though his plump fist with those thick and hairy fingers had given her a quick punch under the ribs.

There must be an error, she heard herself whisper. Paul Kingwood Johnson?

Paul Kingwood Johnson, afterwards married to Amy Ferrier, now deceased. Two children were in fact born to Amy Johnson, but both are now living abroad and, although they have been contacted, are unwilling to have him live with them. I understand they did not get on, a certain amount of bad feeling on all sides. Mr Johnson himself speaks rather bitterly of them, no doubt on account of the extremity of his situation, being so frail. And he is hardly fit enough to travel to another country, even if he were willing and we had the jurisdiction.

And of us? How does he speak of us?

Edith had not used this personal pronoun to link herself to her brother in years, perhaps not since they were both small children. But now they were suddenly one flesh. This father, or non-father, whoever he might be, had surpassed Robert in wrongdoing: his deceit, or betrayal, whichever it might be, put Robert in a better light, so he seemed merely venal, human. It could be thought, and Edith had often thought it, that his weaknesses were wholly or in part due to his father's absence, and if his father had chosen to absent himself, then he was certainly culpable.

It was too much, it was confusing, it was clearly absurd.

I don't believe it. Look at the picture. Does he look like a traitor? Or like the person in your charge?

I'm sorry, he said, but there really is no possibility of error. I know this has come as a shock, or you would not expect an old man – and we must all grow old, he added, and shook his head mournfully – to look as he did then, in his finest hour. And his medals are not bogus. DFC with bar, as I recall. Have you no pity for him?

His voice was distinctly reproachful. Leaning forward, he looked full into her eyes. His own were big and black, with a sad expression. If it had been him she had to pity, Edith would have had no difficulty, seeing him peering helplessly out of his obese hummock of flesh, fighting for every lungful of air. But he was not here on his own behalf, and Edith grew tense, resisting.

No. I had a difficult childhood. I owe him nothing. You are telling me that my own mother was deceitful, a liar. What do you expect?

She drew herself up to her full height, spitting the

73

words out. The effrontery of this man, or rather, of the authority from which he came, rendered her almost speechless, so she had difficulty in phrasing a formal response.

Her visitor was finding his task awkward, as she could discern. Sweat was trickling down his fat cheeks, and he kept dabbing it off, his hand now trembling visibly. Edith did not wish to hurry him unduly, but she was also afraid he might be taken ill at any moment. Now, to her discomfiture, he began stammering.

N-no n-need to d-do anything r-right away. His arms shook as he attempted to heave his weight from out of a sitting position. Y-you will w-want to think about it, c-consider your p-position. Th-that's only natural.

He had achieved a standing posture, and with it a more assured speech delivery.

Here's my card. You can ring this number in office hours.

He took control of his capacious body and staggered to the door.

It had begun to rain once more, but insidiously now, softly and steadily, a cool whisper in the trees, a misty veil falling continuously, but soon the steady drip drip was sounding indoors, softly now, first in her own bedroom, then in her mother's. Each leak had its own rhythm, beginning to argue now in irregular counterpoint. It was disturbing, but not enough to expel her own disturbing thoughts. Perhaps it was just an echo of what was going on in her own head: until now she had visualised the past as solid, firm, not a pleasing structure, but reliable. Now it was falling down, supports unsteady, each angle crazy. She could no longer negotiate a way through it, for even the ground plan of the familiar was obscured by debris, crumbling masonry. She had seen solid houses unexpectedly destroyed during the war, shattered by a bomb in the night or, even more shockingly, struck by a rocket falling out of a clear sky, in broad daylight. But she had not thought that the past could be wrecked so long after the final 'all clear', with her childhood and the war a dim but historic memory.

But where was her mother in all this? It brought back a recurring nightmare of her schooldays: Edith would be running through the streets, dragging her satchel, after she heard the explosion, saw the column of black smoke rising above nearby rooftops, the frantic thud of her heart only slowing down when she saw that their house was still there. But now there would be no such reassurance, she could not turn the corner, walk up the garden path and turn the key in the lock, find the familiar figure shaking a tablecloth out of the back door, doing what she usually did at that hour of the day. Edith felt she no longer knew what she did, or anything about her. If she had been buried under rubble, she could not have told the rescuers in their tin helmets who to look for in the wreckage.

Only for a Muriel Johnson who had apparently spent her life lying to those around her, with whom she lived on a day-to-day basis, who had since spun a web of deceit stretching over a half a century, who was suspected of profound hypocrisy. She had forgiven her shortcomings on the grounds that she was a bit stupid, but apparently she was all devious complexity, her soul a maze, mysterious as it was misleading.

This had not been an impromptu falsehood, if such it

was, spoken in the confusion of the moment, and later hard to undo. It could scarcely be considered kind to let them think their father was dead, rather than simply absent. No, Muriel Johnson could only have been thinking of herself. She had clung to the fallacious dignity of being a war widow, rather than confess to being a deserted wife. The failure of divorce was simply not admissible.

Fury overwhelmed her when she recalled how she had been brought up as an offering to Hymen, as surely as any ancient king had sacrificed his daughter to the gods of war. If her feet had not been bound, if she had escaped actual mutilation from the surgeon's knife, nevertheless attempts went on constantly to push her to this destiny. From the first blood-letting when she was thirteen Mrs Johnson had spared no effort to stunt her natural growth, constrain her instincts, divert her from all enthusiasms unconnected with domesticity or personal grooming. Her shortcomings had been her mother's triumph, for had not her parent already achieved this apotheosis through matrimony? In the years of her ageing spinsterhood Mrs Johnson never failed to take the opportunity of commenting on her daughter's lack of success.

If Edith's hair would not curl, or her custard went lumpy, it was interpreted as an ill augury. Later, on visits home, minor promotions at the office were of less interest than the presence of eligible bachelors in the department, or her dating habits after hours. And, when her figure had irredeemably thickened, the hair on her head begun to go grey, the reproaches flew like arrows, each dart tipped with the venom of triumph. I told you so. But would she listen? For Edith's cronies were quite likely to be drawn in, as she lamented Edith's failure to provide her with grandchildren, or the hardship of being left a war widow with a young family.

Edith would have found all this less hard to bear if she had felt utterly content, without unfulfilled longings or secret regrets. Not that she had ever for a moment felt impelled to follow her mother's instructions or strive for her goals. She found her prescriptions, her view of the world, ridiculously simplistic. But she also knew that her present situation was the result, not of choice, but of necessity. If she had had her way it would all have been different, there would have been a loving husband, and several children. She knew that there had never been a moment when she might have taken a different turning, and so been happy. She knew that what she had mostly been offered was a whole series of wrong turnings, which she had sensibly refused to take. She might not have been lucky, but at least she had been sturdy enough not to run for cover, accept the odd dubious proposal, take shelter behind a surburban privet hedge. No, she could only identify one juncture at which she might have chosen differently, for good or ill, but she had not known at the time just what a void she would be left with, that there was to be no second chance. And, even if she had known, would she have had the inner resource to go through with it, and keep the child?

Mrs Johnson knew nothing of the abortion, and Edith found a deep, if bitter, pleasure in thinking of her mother's lasting discomfiture if she had given birth to a bastard. Now she found herself laughing, not at this old notion, which could still hurt her physically: she was laughing with relief, because her mother had been found out. From early childhood Edith had been taught to

77

worship an image, sacrifice each and every gift she might possess at its shrine, follow the path of duty as interpreted by its high priestess. Now, it seemed, the high priestess had been lying all along, the god was a deceiving god, an idol with feet of clay under the gilding.

·9·

Signs of autumn were visible, though summer lingered on, touching the world with fading colours of antique gold, a dying presence unwilling to let go. But the nights got dark quickly, and in the cool mist of early morning a fresh cohort of small children could be seen marching off to school in new uniforms, hung around with stiff satchels, still empty. The trees had burnt themselves out, tired green turning yellow and brittle brown, and the pavements were littered with their droppings.

Quarterly rent demands came through with the falling leaves, sure as the turning seasons, and accepted with the same glum fatalism as imminent winter. But this quarter had the tenants rather less acquiescent. Nobody paid willingly, everybody thought it unjust. Edith's roof was still leaking: a workman went up through the skylight and told her the job could not be done without scaffolding, and since then she had heard nothing. Jane Lamb had a serious damp problem, a distinctly awful smell in her rooms. Mrs

Gardiner complained loud and long about her creaking floorboards and rotting windows, although she had least to worry about in the relative security of the raised ground floor. She was also refusing to pay the service charges, so she told Edith, since nobody had cleaned the common parts for over a month.

Edith kept writing letters, each more forthright than the last, the terminology a bit more legalistic, as she got no reply. Winter was imminent, she told the landlord, the weather would worsen, soon there would be no possibility of working on the roof, rain or snow could bring down her ceilings. She also wrote on behalf of Rhoda, too listless to draft anything, about her plumbing. Jane Lamb, meanwhile, had been snatching free moments off work to seek legal advice, much of which was provided free. But it was not encouraging. Although a landlord undoubtedly had a statutory duty to carry out essential repairs, it was difficult to get the law enforced. This could take, not months, but years. The authority had a statutory duty to act, but was at present seriously understaffed through lack of funds, and already had a vast backlog. As things stood, officers could only deal with the most serious cases, and at present they would not fall in that category. Taking all this into account, she was told, her best course was to go on pressing the landlord herself, preferably in conjunction with other tenants.

It was not what she wanted to hear but at least, now, they knew where they stood. Edith spent a good deal of time trying to get through on the telephone, and Jane also tried, either in the lunch hour or when she got back from school, but neither of them managed to contact the landlord. Together they had a chat with Mrs Gardiner, but found her unhelpful. Although she had long been in the habit of boasting of her solicitor, a status symbol denied to less privileged persons, referring to him constantly, she did not, rather to Edith's surprise, offer to consult him now. On the contrary, as the two women emphasised the urgency of the situation, and the necessity of acting in unison, Mrs Gardiner began to contradict herself, backtracking on her previous propensity to complain about defects in the building.

The two women agreed not to contact Rhoda, who was too ill to exert herself, or the Wolfs, clearly far too nervous of stirring up trouble, of alien forces ready to engulf them. Even getting through to them would be problematic.

The weather was worsening, with more water leaking through the roof. Edith found the situation depressing. She was also annoyed at Mrs Gardiner's continuing complaints, now that she had so blatantly refused to help herself, or her neighbours, in trying to get defects in the building rectified. Far from being shamefaced, Mrs Gardiner had apparently put the incident out of her mind, behaving as if she bore no responsibility for any inconvenience she might be suffering. She continued to pry into Edith's post, to waylay her in the hall, either to give her opinion of the world, its rapid decline into barbarism, or to decry her cleaning woman, her absence, her tardiness, her unreliability.

As for Rhoda, to visit her was discouraging. She was either lying in bed or slopping round in a dressing gown, her skin wrinkling like a leaky balloon with loss of weight. It was not just that she was not improving, Edith had begun to doubt her mental stability. She spoke darkly about foreigners living next door, referring to the Wolfs, and how she suspected them of getting rid of Felix. She now had an obsession about Felix, his vanishing. The following morning it was suddenly Mrs Gardiner who had always objected to Felix, and who must therefore have put poison in a saucer of milk. Edith, afraid that she herself might become the object of suspicion, did not try to argue with her. Nor did she attempt to inform her about the leaking roof, rising damp in the basement or signs of subsidence.

On a morning of autumnal mist Edith got up as usual. Dragging herself out of bed, this burdensome weight, she put on a dressing gown and went wearily into the kitchen, aching, her head still numb. She lit the gas under the kettle and glanced out at the dull sky, wondering, as she so often did at this hour, how much longer she would be going through this diurnal routine. It had been going on for so long.

She yawned, stretched, poured boiling water into the teapot, then turned off the gas. The grey sky did not look threatening, merely boring. The summer birds had departed, now the stay-at-homes in their dreary feathers sat about in trees almost bereft of leaf. Raucous rooks were invading their branches, the misty sky. Soon she would need to worry about the cold. Edith was about to turn away from the window and pour her first cup of the morning when she saw something below, out of the corner of her eye, then fully, which disrupted every reflex action, dispelled every foggy thought.

Down below stood a FOR SALE sign. She thought it must be an error, that it signified the house next door, but no, it was firmly attached to the brick gatepost of this building. She went on staring, in shock and disbelief. Amidst all her petty concerns, her quotidian anxieties, she had not been expecting this. The possibility had not so much as occurred to her. The blow had struck without warning.

Edith let her tea grow cold. She kept going to her bedroom to dress, only to return to the kitchen, look down at the sign yet again. As if she could not believe her own eyes. Thoughts going through her mind had no focus, cloudy, shifting aimlessly. She put on a grey skirt, took it off. Not knowing why she had changed her mind, she put it on again. For reasons she could not fathom Edith kept connecting the estate agent's sign with the mystery of the man purporting to be her father. Then she understood there was no reason, no link, except that both events had been utterly unexpected, and neither could fit into her scheme of things, be accommodated into her universe without destroying it. She was struck by the absurdity of her efforts to keep an orderly control of her surroundings: seeing the pans still half full of rainwater at strategic points on the floors provoked a mirthless snigger. Each and every strategy was, after all, a form of futility.

Apparently she was not the only person struck by the unexpected shock. She found the Wolfs sitting on the stairs, a few steps below their landing. They seemed careless of who might see them, distraught. He was comforting her, touching and caressing like an elderly husband. Edith found herself embarrassed at seeing them, after all their attempts at secrecy. She felt like a voyeur. Martha Wolf was visibly shaking, her dry leaf of a body crumbling under his touch, which was vague, fumbling, but infinitely tender. Thinking she had seen something not meant for her, and which she would have preferred not to witness, for it was also painful, she turned to go back upstairs with as little noise as possible. If they heard her go, neither gave any sign.

So what? What difference does it make to us?

Rhoda did not even bother to go to the window and see for herself. Slumped in an armchair, she put her head back and shut her eyes. Her grey hair was unkempt, and a sweetish sour odour came from the dingy dressing gown. The room, despite Edith's help, was once more in disorder. Dirty cups stood on the coffee table, garments lay draped over the backs of chairs.

We have our rights, she went on wearily, eyes still firmly shut. But the remark seemed to amuse her, for the ghost of a smile curled her lip. And nobody is going to do us any favours.

She lifted her head and opened her eyes, looking intently at Edith, who saw irises now almost bereft of colour. I don't care who owns the bloody place.

Edith felt that she was beyond help, and undoubtedly beyond helping. She got up to go. She had no spirit, this morning, to water Rhoda's drooping pot plants or tidy up her kitchen. As she was moving to the door she heard Rhoda saying behind her: Did you kill Felix?

Edith hurried into the passage, thinking it best to say nothing. Her old friend was not herself. In the corridor, edging past the rucksack, she heard Rhoda shouting: But I think you know who did.

Outside, on the landing, she heard voices arguing, loudly, their pitch full of anger. They were speaking in a foreign language, so she could not make out specific words and phrases, but both timbre and tempo suggested an exchange of charge and counter-charge, furiously accusing. She stood for a moment, listening, frustrated at not being able to eavesdrop properly. She knew it was wrong to do so, but this had never prevented her, curiosity being so strong.

Mrs Gardiner was standing on the front steps, looking fixedly at the estate agent's sign. She was unexpectedly calm about it.

I'm not altogether surprised, she told Edith, with enviable composure, fiddling with the pearls strung round her neck. You only have to look at his shirts, to say nothing of the way he neglects this place, to know he is not a man of means.

Edith found herself almost admiring her sang-froid, Mrs Gardiner's hauteur, the way she simply looked down on anybody without unlimited assets. Though it had often infuriated her in the past.

The odd thing is, Edith told her, it's apparently under offer. I rang up the agent, pretending to be a potential buyer.

Mrs Gardiner suddenly looked at her in a manner Edith found disquieting.

Yes, well, she said evasively, turning to go into the house, I have been considering my position. Naturally. My lawyer is advising me.

Edith was left to wonder, and worry. The very notion of Mrs Gardiner becoming the proprietor was annoying and rather absurd: there would be no end of petty harassment and minor tyranny.

*

The stiff signboard outside was horribly conspicuous, blatant battle colours nailed to the gatepost, and it never seemed to be quite out of the periphery of her vision. Edith had decided that, if anybody came to inspect the house, she would refuse entry to her part of it. She had only to see a passer-by glance at the billboard to feel her heart pounding. She had not thought beyond this point, but she knew she had rights, and nothing in the world would induce her to open the front door to an army of squalid speculators. If the landlord arrived at the house with a prospective buyer, she would give him a piece of her mind. At least the tenants should have been notified, it was only proper, they should not have the roof sold over their heads without prior notice, or the opportunity of buying it themselves. The fact that neither she nor, as far as she knew, any of the tenants, with the possible exception of Mrs Gardiner, had enough money to buy the property, this had been conveniently consigned to the back of her mind. She dimly felt that, acting in concord, they might somehow have found a way of controlling their own destiny, finding a solution. She vaguely recalled some such plan, years ago, when there was some doubt about the ownership of the premises, and there had been much discussion about the possibility of a collective purchase. Edith was not sure just why the plan had fizzled out, but as far as she could remember it had been from collective indecision rather than the lack of a specific sum. If her memory was correct, they had never got down to naming a sum, or asking for it. Nevertheless, it might still not be too late to try. If anybody could get the thing going, set it in motion, it would be Jane Lamb.

Edith felt jumpy, besieged. She kept peering nervously out of the front windows, listening fearfully for a ring at her door.

In the evening, when Edith did finally see Jane, she found herself feeling more uneasy than hitherto. She had gone down to the basement, and at first could get no reply. When Jane came to the door, she was unexpectedly curt.

Look, I really can't stop now. Some other time.

Edith felt apologetic, but also hurt. In all the years she had known her, Jane had never spoken so abruptly. Something, she felt, was bothering her. Brooding afterwards, into the small hours of morning, she kept wondering whether she had done something to offend her, but could think of nothing. Perhaps some personal crisis, or disturbing knowledge she did not wish to share? Unanswered questions loomed large in the dark, and she slept badly.

. 10 .

The days grew short, darkness falling earlier each night. Severe gales stripped the trees of their last leaves, also took off a few branches. Edith began to think her fears were perhaps unfounded: as far as she knew nobody had come to view the house, and she was not asked to give access to strangers. The billboard blew down in the night, giving Edith a momentary spurt of joy the following morning. But her pleasure was short-lived: it was immediately replaced by a sign saying SOLD.

She saw nobody with whom she could discuss the situation. Her relationship with Rhoda had turned chilly, now that the latter had begun rewarding good deeds with insults. Edith knew she was ill, but nevertheless found it hard to accept so much venomous suspicion. She had not been to see her for almost a week, and the longer she put off visiting her, the harder it was to go through with it. As for the Wolfs, they had resumed their former invisibility, nor had Edith heard a sound from their flat recently.

When she thought of them, and in her mind they had become birds, she wondered whether they had finally flown, impelled by some blind instinct of panic. She had dreamt of them, turning into snow geese, winging in unison with shrill cries over an icebound country.

She had begun spying on Mrs Gardiner since the SOLD sign was put up, coming down early in the morning in order to look at her incoming post. Any qualms she might have felt at such conduct were dispelled by the knowledge that her victim had been doing just this for years. But Mrs Gardiner's letters seemed to be mostly bills, many with the colour of urgency about them. She wondered whether, as a result of some major financial undertaking, such as purchasing the house, her neighbour had got temporarily behind with the payment of routine bills, or whether she was simply getting absent-minded in her old age. She hung about, now and then, hoping to see her, for a bit of revealing gossip.

But Mrs Gardiner kept within doors. She had recently had a bad fall, tripping over an unmended paving stone. Edith, though regretting the accident, was mindful of the irony. Mrs Gardiner was always saying that local taxes were daylight robbery and, though she was also loudly vocal on the hazardous condition of the pavements, the potholes, the loose and broken stones, saw no connection between falling taxes and falling down. Anyhow, she had fallen headlong, and was lucky, given her advanced age, to get away with severe bruising, a few grazes and a twisted ankle. She might easily have had a fracture, a serious condition for the elderly.

If immobility made it easy to pry through her post with impunity, Edith found this unsatisfactory, now that the

SOLD sign had gone up, and was hoping for something more concrete from her neighbour's lips. She felt that, if Mrs Gardiner was involved in the purchase of the house, triumph would soon bring her out, hobbling painfully on her walking stick, and thought, going downstairs, it might be this morning. Through the landing window she saw the sign swaying in the wind, plastic blowing skyward. And, if not triumph, then overriding curiosity.

But Edith never reached the ground floor. Suddenly she found herself confronting a dog, black, immense, sitting on the first landing, watching her with unflinching eyes. A kind of incredulity swept through her, so if she froze, hand on bannister, left foot poised for the next step, it was, at first, less from terror than disbelief. She thought she must be hallucinating, dreaming. She had heard no sound, and heard nothing now: the creature merely continued to sit on its haunches, still, alert, watchful.

She told herself: this is surrealism. The sight had no logic, no similarity to anything that had ever happened here, no link with expectation of any kind. She could only think of a fairy tale from her childhood, in which black dogs came out of the ether when a tinderbox was lit. This absurd link simply made her feel even more helpless, more foolish. She had no magic tool, and was not living in a fairy tale.

His eyes had begun to shift, and she glimpsed bloodshot rims. It was sinister, that his eyes should have no whites, nothing human about him. Now he was lowering his massive head, muzzle quivering, picking up her odour. A mauvish tongue quickly flicked across his jaws, revealing the pale inner flesh.

Still no sound, though dimly in the background Edith

could hear normality. From Mrs Gardiner's kitchen the thin tinkle of silver and porcelain, from beyond the house the usual surge of traffic flowing in irregular tidal motion. But now a profound growl had begun to issue from the black depths of him, a kind of tremor lightly touching his skin, rippling, an undercurrent of power.

Edith found herself going up the stairs, backwards, very slowly, cautiously, not taking her eyes off him. She had begun to do so even before the animal got up, stood upright. As soon as the bannister obstructed her vision of him she had an instinctive, overwhelming urge to turn round and run, but did not do so. She knew that to show fear was the worst thing, that it could smell her and, even out of sight, its hearing would be acute. She had seen him prick up his ears, his head turning to watch her go. So she went up as steadily as she knew how, hoping, though her heart was pounding, that his hearing might interpret this steadiness as calm. Nor did she turn round, knowing it was vital to keep her eye on anything that could still be seen, and that victory had to do with outfacing the threatening other in the animal kingdom. And then, the thought of being attacked from behind was terrifying.

For whatever reason, the dog did not follow her. Either she had done the correct thing, or it was not after her, not now. Edith got to the top landing and, very quietly and cautiously, stepped through her own front door, shutting it firmly. Then she began to tremble, leaning against the solid wood, fighting for breath. Her entire weight was against the door, as if the animal might try to batter it down, or she herself needed propping up. But she heard nothing, only her own laborious breathing, and the thud in her chest.

Edith stood leaning against the door for almost half an hour. After her pulse and breathing had settled down she found the stillness beyond the door not so much reassuring as eerie. She thought she might be ill, that perhaps she was suffering from delusions: first a man saying that her father was still living, now this dreadful dog. Teach us to expect the unexpected, this she had heard somewhere, and the words re-entered her mind now. She could not mistrust her five senses, if living was not to become an impossibility.

So, in the following hours, Edith felt herself under siege. She had intended to go out of doors. Instead she padded anxiously from room to room, peering out of windows for portents, putting her ear to the front door for any sounds beyond it. She thought of calling the police but did not do so, fearful that they would regard her as a batty old thing making a fuss about nothing. And if they did come round, and found no dog sitting on the landing, then they would certainly think her mad. Or accuse her of wasting their time. No, she was undergoing a siege and must sit it out. She reckoned that sooner or later the dog, which also had animal instincts, would go off to satisfy them.

Towards dusk she opened her front door with extreme caution, trying to make no sound, and tiptoed down, peering over the bannister at intervals. As she expected, there was no sign of the dog.

. II .

The next morning the Lambs' cocker spaniel was found
hanging in the back garden. Edith did not actually see it
herself: by the time she drew back the bedroom curtains
the body had been cut down, and all she saw was a small
group standing under the tree, surrounding a crouching
figure. Almost prostrate, Chris was kneeling on the
muddy grass, fondling something that at first looked no
more than a limp rag, but after a moment she made out the
dim red-gold of his coat, and knew it to be his pet dog. It
had grown darker over the years, the dog growing old as
the boy grew up; now it was lying still under the tree, and
the boy's posture, also the way the ad hoc group around
him was watching, made Edith hurry downstairs in her
dressing gown and slippers.

The last remnants of morning mist still clung to the bare
trees, and the damp lawn was strewn with shed leaves,
their colour now dull as the dog lying on the ground. The
group stood around the weeping boy in an odd collection

93

of clothing, day and nightwear, apparently struck dumb by such grief, such unexpectedly vicious behaviour. Helpless looks met hers as she trod over the tarnished leaves in her furry slippers, and even the boy's mother seemed at a loss, struck by a curious kind of immobility. Edith saw her hands hovering, but not quite touching the boy's fair head, his shaking shoulders, as though she knew there was nothing she could do to comfort him, no easy benediction. He must grow up now, on his own.

The dog's head was lying at an unnatural angle, and now Edith saw the length of rope tied round its neck. The dog had grown stout this last year or two, and, ambling about the neighbourhood on a slack lead, sniffing at lampposts without urgency, was far from being the frisky puppy Chris had once been given. Chris, being an intelligent boy, knew his time was running out, even if he did not know how to deal with it. Jane, Edith knew, had been dropping hints, with a view to preparing him. But not for such barbarity. Nothing in her vocabulary, in her upbringing of the boy, had taken such a thing into account, or could account for it.

Luckily, if it is possible to speak of luck, the house did hold a tenant who was all too familiar with this form of human conduct, its dark springs and shocking aftermath. It needed a foreigner, perhaps, to comprehend anything so alien. Fred Wolf came striding across the lawn, pursued by Martha, hesitant and stumbling. Few had seen him through the years, and nobody had seen him so self-possessed. Several of the neighbours had no notion who he was, and even those who did were taken aback by his lack of diffidence.

Take him indoors, he said firmly, lifting the distraught

boy by the shoulders. Hot sweet tea, he added, as Martha put her arms round Chris. She led him towards the house, with Jane hurrying after. Fetch a spade, he barked, almost glaring at a dumb-struck neighbour, who had never seen him up till now. Well, what are you waiting for? We must bury the dog.

The neighbour worked his jaw up and down several times, but no sound came out. Right, he said at last. Right you are. And hurried off in his dressing gown, a civilian obeying orders in a sudden emergency.

Why? Why? Why would someone do a thing like that?

Edith could hear the boy's voice, suddenly high and childish, rising plaintively near the house.

Martha was comforting him. Hush, she said soothingly, still holding him. The world is full of evil, and wicked people.

And Jane was now looking utterly helpless. Edith had never seen her face so grey and chalky, eyes void of colour. If she was resentful of Martha Wolf's sudden influence, words which went against her own teaching, then she could do nothing to stop it.

Afterwards nobody mentioned the incident, or thought to discuss it. Edith had lingered in the garden whilst the dog was being buried, then went away silently. She did not look out of her back windows, but kept seeing the tiny mound of fresh brown earth. She guessed that neither Chris nor his mother had gone off to their respective schools, but could not bring herself to visit them. Her normal instinct would have been to hurry down to the basement and offer such crumbs of comfort as she could find, but this outrage did not fit into the category of normal. She felt it was best to leave them alone for now. And something in Jane's expression had deterred her too, an alien and unexpected look which Edith found forbidding. No doubt she was angry, rightly so, but Edith could have sworn the look she saw expressed hatred, a deeply felt enmity to the surrounding world. This was so utterly foreign to the person she had known for so long that it put her off going.

But she did visit the Lambs towards the end of the week. The nights were dark early now, and Edith found the lights on the staircase did not work. Only fitful light through the landing windows, throwing long shadows. Edith felt her way down uneasily, step by cautious step, clutching the bannister. Although she knew each creaking tread, every step and turn, she had grown nervous of going down after her confrontation with the huge black dog. He might be there again, at any time, to block her path, terrify her, perhaps attack. Now eerie shadows and dark corners made her descent that much more nerve-racking.

Warm light radiated from the basement windows, and Jane Lamb stood back from the door to let her enter without saying a word. As usual, the sitting room looked chaotic and welcoming, with old newspapers, school exercise books and unwashed mugs strewn on every surface. Jane cleared a space for her to sit down.

I don't know what to say to him. She spoke dully, letting out a sigh. As she sank back on the sofa a pile of exercise books, unbalanced by weight redistribution, lost its equilibrium and slid to the floor. She let them lie.

I don't know what to say to him. Not that it matters, because he won't talk. He shuts himself in his room and just stays there. He thinks it's his fault, that he should have made sure the dog was in his basket. Edith, I think he was. I think I left the back door unlocked, and somebody got in.

She did not speak for a while, but sat looking down at the hands in her lap, fiddling with her fingers, unmanicured and ringless.

Perhaps I've been too trusting. If only they had stolen my purse, or the radio. What should I have done, Edith? I don't believe in molly-coddling a child, I know I should be preparing him for whatever is out there. But I want him to be good, and trusting, and generous. And he is, isn't he, Edith? He's turning out very well, and I'm proud of him.

Her eyes flitted wildly round the room, seeing nothing.

And now this. He thinks I've been lying to him, that there's something I haven't told him. I feel it. But I thought I was telling the truth. I really believe in redemption. What I mean is, if I did not, how could I possibly have brought a child into the world, willingly?

She stared at Edith beseechingly.

But I did, and now my great fear is he will not forgive me.

Edith was struck dumb. She felt as though a well inside her had suddenly run dry. Kept throwing down a bucket but heard only a hollow sound. Yes, she began, and heard metal clanging on stone. She cleared her throat, in which a tiny pebble seemed to have got stuck. It's not your fault, she began, this time with increasing conviction. You always did your best. As you saw it. But now he has to grow up. Edith heard herself speaking, and heard the empty bucket scraping the dry bottom. Whether the woman sitting on the sofa could hear anything, she did not know. Perhaps only the dry sound from the empty bottom.

So Edith abandoned any attempt at words, simply got up to sit beside her. A few remaining exercise books either slid to the floor or were heedlessly crushed. Edith took Jane's hands, two wild and frantic birds, in both of hers and only when she felt them grow calm enough did she let them go.

He says he won't ever have another dog.

Jane spoke as though this loss of faith was too much for her. Dully, she turned to Edith, who saw that her youthful looks had been fading, and were now irreparable. Her skin looked worn by the weather, dry and slack, her loose hair too girlish. This shook Edith, her senior.

He's upset at the moment. He'll get over it.

But Edith, knowing the boy to be intelligent, thought he would not get over it, not enough to acquire a new dog.

. 12 .

The murder of the cocker spaniel overshadowed all other concerns, at least temporarily. It was too shocking, too brutal to be easily put out of mind. The weather was dry, though cold, so Edith did not need to listen out for the nagging sound of the roof leaking. She had taken a bus to the outer suburbs with a bunch of bronze chrysanthemums for her mother, and felt good about it. As for the terrifying dog who had prevented her from going out, there had been no further sighting of him, and Edith was beginning to think it was just a bad dream, or perhaps even a hallucination of some kind.

But if she was imagining things, it was certainly an omen of what was to follow. She realised this when Mrs Gardiner drew her anxiously, almost furtively, into her apartment one morning and claimed that somebody had moved into the empty flat next door to her.

These rooms had been unoccupied for years, and no tenant could remember a time when anyone had lived there. As a result each of them had a theory, if not several, as to why this apartment might have been left empty. Originally, particularly before the present landlord took over, a favourite presumption had been that the owner was keeping it either for himself or for a grown-up child. This had gradually lost credibility, and a much more disturbing theory had by now gained the ascendancy, namely, that the owner was biding his time, and was expecting to get vacant possession of the entire house in the future, for the purpose of selling or demolition. Whether or not the empty rooms had been suffering from rot or decay when the last tenant left, there could be no doubt that they must have deteriorated very seriously since, which was worrying. Mrs Gardiner in particular, living next door, intermittently spoke of wet rot, dry rot, noxious odours, and infestations of mice. Once, during an especially bitter winter, she thought she heard rats. Now and then she also claimed to have heard human beings moving about during the night.

So when Mrs Gardiner grabbed Edith by the arm, drew her into the hallway and told her, whispering, that she had been kept awake half the night by sounds coming through the wall, that she thought a squatter had moved in, Edith's first reaction was to dismiss this story as yet one more symptom of the old woman's recurring anxieties. For Mrs Gardiner had visibly aged during the past few months. She had shrunk slightly, and still walked slowly, leaning heavily on her stick. Her clothes, too, had lost their meticulous grooming, looking crumpled, revealing the odd stain.

Nonsense, retorted Edith impatiently. I expect you were dreaming. But her hostility to this woman was turning to pity, and there was no doubting her terror. Try not to worry.

Edith was halfway up the stairs when she heard a loud crashing sound. It came from below and, there was no doubt about it, from the empty flat. Mrs Gardiner was still standing in her doorway, looking up. She shook with the tremor, letting her walking stick drop. Edith was already hurrying down.

You see, she whispered, her voice querulous. Dreaming? I couldn't sleep a wink all night for terror.

Edith held on to Mrs Gardiner's elbow and pushed her through the door, shutting it firmly. She felt safer for the moment. Mrs Gardiner's hallway was extremely small, since it was simply a minute portion of the original entrance hall, when one family occupied the entire house. Then it had been an imposing residence, constructed for the wealthy.

Come and sit down, she told Mrs Gardiner, pushing her into the living room. She found she was also speaking in a whisper.

Who do you think it is? Ought we to call the police?

Her eyes were round with fright, helpless. She was turning to Edith for support.

Mrs Gardiner, once so pristine, now exuded an odour of stale perfume mingled with other, undefined body smells. Her drawing room was full of knick-knacks, silver miniatures arranged on side tables, china bibelots on glass shelves. The furniture was ornate, with curved backs and curly legs. It was not a room in which anybody could settle comfortably and Edith, who had only rarely been here, found herself perching tentatively on the edge of her antique chair, assessing the objects on display all around.

I thought of calling the police in the night, when I first heard him. Mrs Gardiner was still whispering. But I didn't dare. I thought, if he hears me, he'll murder me right away. You hear such stories. And then the police hardly ever come nowadays, or they take far too long to do anything.

Edith knew that Mrs Gardiner had long been in the habit of ringing the police for trivial reasons, or on the basis of false alarms. Perhaps she had cried wolf too often, so they no longer took any notice.

If there is an intruder, then we must inform them.

Edith thought, but did not go on to say, that it was surprising for it to have taken so long for a homeless person to notice the unoccupied rooms and move in, particularly since the empty flat was on the ground floor. With so many destitutes now roaming the city, sleeping rough, begging even in the suburbs, it was only to be expected. So far, it was true, such unfortunates had tended to avoid respectable residential areas and doss down in abandoned factories, empty warehouses, or in derelict buildings, rat-infested railway sidings, abandoned churches. But Edith knew that this must change, that with a further slide into anarchy the young and strong would find the temerity to break in openly, showing a contempt for property rights. Edith felt this must be so, knowing how she would act in their position.

But Mrs Gardiner would not have understood, so she did not say what she thought. Besides, Edith did not wish to alarm her further. Mrs Gardiner might have deserved to have her world shaken up, half a century ago perhaps; now she was far too old for it. She would simply crumble, becoming pathetic. Edith could see the first signs now, in her trembling hands, the untidy hair and eyes wild with fright. Uncertain what to do, she was looking absently at the porcelain shepherdess near her elbow, the picturesque urchin in his rags, when a sudden crashing sound from beyond the dividing wall shook the glass shelving. The urchin on his tree stump fell to the floor, but miraculously did not shatter.

Meissen! wailed Mrs Gardiner, hurriedly getting up.

This won't do, Edith said firmly, hurrying into the hallway. I'm going to find out just what is going on.

Not giving herself an opportunity to lose her nerve, she went outside into the main hall and knocked on the door of the other flat. Mrs Gardiner was watching nervously from her own threshold, clutching the front door, ready to shut it in a hurry if need be.

Edith stood for a moment, hearing only the thudding of her own heart, then banged on the door a second time, more aggressively. Now she heard footfalls echoing within, a heavy tread on bare boards, and the door which had been unused for so long swung back.

Yer?

He was standing so near to her that she took a step back before really seeing him, from shaven head to bootclad foot. She saw blue shadows in the close-cropped skull, hard watchful eyes, an angular jaw peppered with rough stubble. He was chewing, the jaw lurching slowly from side to side, with relaxed insolence, as he peered down at her from his superior height. He was wearing a brass ring in his left ear, and his leather clothing had studs and chains on it, a conspicuous display. His hands, too, had rings on the dirty tattooed fingers, but it was the massive black dog he held back by its heavy studded collar which drew Edith's eyes. She had seen him before, and the dog knew it. It had begun to growl, pulling forward.

Yer? Whatcher want?

He went out of his way, by the way he stood, the nonchalant manner in which he went on chewing, to show that he was totally indifferent to her. His hand, however, was still restraining the dog. For the moment.

I want to know what you are doing here.

Edith stood her ground with difficulty. She could feel the dog's wet muzzle sniffing at her skirt and, although she attempted to speak firmly, almost did not recognise the voice coming out as hers. It was oddly high, squeaky. Her sense of security was further undermined when she heard Mrs Gardiner quietly shutting her front door. She was on her own now.

Whazzat ter do with yoo?

The dog was growling more loudly now, and his owner bent down to stroke him. Edith saw a snake tattoo on his index finger, and a heavy ring depicting a skull and crossbones. As he was bending forward she also saw a small red scar on his scalp.

It has everything to do with me. Edith was now relying on her dignity. I live here.

Do yer? Well, so do I now, see? Satisfied? He was almost sneering, looking her up and down with overt contempt.

No. I think you are trespassing.

His heavy leather-clad body was blocking the doorway, but Edith tried to see past him into the interior of the flat for signs, whether of transience or legality. She only caught a glimpse of dirty walls, a dusty ceiling, and a naked light bulb hanging from it.

Nosy, aren't yer? Want me and my pal 'ere to show yoo rahnd?

The dog had begun to pant, showing wet gums and an eager tongue. His owner, far from stepping back, moved closer, propping his free arm against the jamb.

I think not, Edith said stiffly, retreating slightly. I could call the police.

Please yerself. But it won't do no good. I've got as much right ter be 'ere as you 'ave. P'raps more.

He was beginning to shut the door, pulling back his animal by the collar.

That dog hasn't. Edith was almost shouting now, determined not to be ousted. Pets – how absurd the word sounded! – aren't allowed. It's against the rules.

Is that so? Whot a shame, eh Bouncer? Well, I've got news for yoo, missus. Them rules 'ave bin changed, see?

He suddenly slammed the door so forcefully that Edith felt herself struck by a gust of air.

· 13 ·

Edith was suffering bad dreams, not just now and then, but every night. She could remember enough in the morning to know they had been bad, and woke up feeling unrested. Also, she could recall enough to know the dreams were of the recurring kind, even whilst she slept she recognised events and scenes, knew she was dreaming, knew what was about to occur, as though she were reliving a purgatorial cycle. This did not disturb her unduly, it was when she thought she was not asleep that the dreams became truly frightening. She took to thinking she was waking up in the night, in her own room, her own bed, to find herself staring up, not at her ceiling, but directly at the night sky, dark and cold, with a sprinkling of very distant stars. The roof above her was a jagged hole, but there was no rubble lying on or around her, so she knew it had not been a bomb, she was not in the war. Nor did there seem to be a storm, the sky and the room and the world beyond were utterly silent, an eerie stillness all around. She might begin to feel icy cold, so frozen that she was totally unable to move her limbs, or begin to feel vertiginous, looking up into the unending depths of night sky, not knowing whether she was spinning or if it was the sky turning, or even if she was looking up or down. A variant of the dream had her cowering under the bedclothes as a loud clap of thunder struck overhead, heavy clouds bursting. Or, in utter stillness, snow would drift down, falling thickly to cover her, and everything in the room. Or the snow would turn to feathers.

During daylight hours Edith was now uneasy: nervous of venturing beyond her front door, on tenterhooks within. If she did have to go out she made cautious preparations, listening out for sounds down below, ever ready to retreat if she felt the coast might not be clear. The man clad in black leather had not left the ground floor, and his comings and goings were unpredictable. As for his animal, his presence was even more of a conundrum. Occasionally he was seen roaming loose in the street or near the dustbins; frequently his owner left him in the main hall at any hour of the day or night. Admittedly the dog was usually chained up, with his leash looped round the newel post at the foot of the stairs, but this could not be depended on. Besides, the leash was not short enough to stop the dog attacking anybody trying to pass. On the contrary, it simply ensured that the animal was bound to inflict his pent-up frustration in just this way.

This loss of liberty brought her unexpectedly closer to Mrs Gardiner, dissolving her previous hostility. For it was Mrs Gardiner who was suffering most from the intruder, and who was always only too ready to discuss the situation. Far from being standoffish now, she had not merely lost her lofty manner, but was obviously frightened, and clung to Edith at every opportunity. She would lurk behind her front door, peering out, the safety chain strung across, only slipping it off briefly to let Edith in, then double lock the door.

She was hardly sleeping, she told Edith, who saw the shadows of fatigue under her eyes. Her colour was bad now, the cheeks hollow. The dreadful man next door kept irregular hours, often sleeping during the day, then up and noisy at night. Mrs Gardiner had heard hammering, footsteps coming and going, loud music. She also heard bizarre sounds, even more terrifying because she could think of no explanation. The black dog would begin, not simply barking, not even whining, but a high-pitched squealing as though it was going through agony, was being systematically tormented. As for its owner, he was either evil or demented, she could hear him laugh out loud, bawling odd words. At other times, when the dog was silent, she heard him gabbling a long, breathless mono-logue, rising and falling, going on and on. She could not catch the gist of what he was saying, but he seemed to be talking to himself.

Edith now went daily into Mrs Gardiner's drawing room, sitting in the midst of its old-world elegance for hours, listening to her neighbour. Until now she had been impatient of the older woman's burden of complaints on the decline of civilised values; besides, until now she would not have been invited in. But for Edith it was slightly reassuring to hear everything, pick up each clue, and discuss the consequences, known and unknown, of this mystery. Such an unexpected event had thrown her, and she had no mechanism for coping with it.

Edith found it diverting to sit on Mrs Gardiner's velvet sofa and look at the pretty ornaments all round her. They had an air of self-assurance, serenity almost, as though asserting intrinsic niceties. She could gaze at rustic landscapes in their gilded frames, stroke the lid of a painted box, express surprise at the patient workmanship in a silver miniature. Mrs Gardiner seemed to appreciate her willingness to stay for a bit, setting out gilded teacups and a sugar bowl with silver tongs whilst the kettle simmered in the kitchen. Now that Mrs Gardiner had lost her former hauteur she seemed glad of a bit of company, and obviously found it comforting to discuss what was troubling them both. Edith felt she was doing a good deed by helping an elderly person.

It was also a form of procrastination. For the first time that she could remember, Edith felt she was not in control. Up till now she had managed well enough, though with difficulty, but suddenly she was quite out of her depths. She did not know what was going on, so felt uncertain how to act. From morning till night she would dither, worry whether she had sufficient food, whether it was prudent to go out, or necessary. When she did go she was nervous about getting back in, expecting she knew not what within the main door. The least disturbing sound from down below, a door shutting, the dog barking, would stop her in her tracks at the point of leaving. She told herself it was about to rain, and took off the coat she had only just put on.

And Edith was sleeping badly, adding to her indecision. It was not just the disturbing dreams, she now found it hard to drop off. Lying alert for hours, she heard, or thought she heard, weird sounds: odd thuds which shook the house during the still night, or a sudden cracking of timber; a high-pitched howl coming from the ground floor or, now and then, creeping footsteps ascending the main stairs. This was the worst, for Edith felt she must be imagining them. The harder they were to hear, the more anxiously she listened for their stealthy, almost inaudible tread, until the wild drumming in her chest drove out all other sounds.

Then she began to get mysterious telephone calls in the night, invariably after she had got off to sleep. On the first occasion Edith was startled out of her first, deepest sleep in the small hours. Hello, she mumbled huskily, after switching on her bedside lamp and peering dazedly at the alarm clock. But found she was listening intently to a vacuum, a humming stillness coming through the dark into her receiver. Eventually she put it down, switched the light off, and slept.

An hour later it rang again. Edith sat bolt upright in bed and began shouting angrily.

Who is this? What the hell do you think you're playing at? Do you know what time it is?

Hearing nothing, she took the receiver from her ear and glared at it, then slammed it into the cradle. She had only just extinguished her lamp when the ringing recommenced. Thinking fury must be the wrong tactic, she attempted a cajoling tone.

Look, she said kindly, if you've got something to say, then say it. I'm listening. Even if it is the middle of the night. I'm wide awake now, so you might as well.

She heard a click, then the continuing purr of dis-engagement.

During the following nights Edith experimented with

every kind of response when the ringing occurred. Please, wheedling, I'm old and ugly, give it a rest. Harshly: don't think you can get away with this, they are on to you, the call's being traced. Or firmly: don't think it bothers me, I'm not frightened of you. As far as she could tell, it changed nothing, the caller was utterly indifferent to the manner in which she reacted, whether she let out a flood of words or said nothing. It might have been a ghost in the machine, a mechanical blip ringing her number, but Edith felt, no, knew, a human agency was behind it. When she was half numb with fatigue she thought she heard breathing, but so tenuous, it was rather the holding of breath, and this she knew, in her waking hours, to be absurd.

She was tired from lack of sleep throughout the day, since the ringing usually began in the small hours, and occurred several times during the night. Even when it did not happen, she usually woke in the night with palpitations, after dreaming she had heard the ringing sound. She kept trying to put a face to the mystery caller, but nothing was convincing, no human eye, no mouth would fix itself in her imagination, known or unknown. Nor could she determine whether the attention being focussed on her now was evidence of loving or hating. But perhaps, if there was no human agency behind the ringing, if it was the mechanism, then she was merely projecting human values into the vacuum, into a vast, mysterious sphere where such things were absent.

Sleepless, Edith listened to the night. Being so high up, she could hear the wind, the rafters creaking. Now the weather was turning wintry, night storms shook the building. In the roof space she heard a regular tapping, and, with the wind rising, her bed itself would begin to sway very slightly. When sleep overtook her during a storm she saw leafless trees writhing in the wind, lost souls blowing through the night sky, torn shreds tossing and turning, the tapping sound was her father's walking stick at the window.

No, she heard herself mutter, turning her weight in the bed. He was a naked tree, twisting bare branches with clawlike twigs, cruciform, dead flesh or living wood, maybe both, but such a wind could tear him up by the roots, flinging him through the window. The high wind screeching through the cracks and rifts in the building, now the shriek was turning into words. Let me in, the words kept whistling shrilly. It could have been a flying spirit, or simply the wind, but by now she was sure it was a child pleading. She was turning her weight to and fro, trying to shut out the sound, when she heard the entry buzzer sounding in the hall. It was a real sound, persisting, and woke Edith up.

Thinking it was morning, she drew back the curtain, but it was still dark. Much too early for the postman, who rang the bell if he could not push a parcel through the letter slot. Yawning, Edith shoved her feet into downtrodden slippers and shuffled into the dark hallway. Hullo? She was beginning to feel cold. Through the receiver of the entryphone system she could hear only the hollow, ghostly sound of the night city. Now and then a solitary car speeding out of the dark, then back into it, the sound dying to nothing.

Edith was perplexed. Her doorbell was occasionally rung by a prankster, a gang of youths roaming the neighbourhood. But not in the small hours of the morning. Foreigners, perhaps also the victims of pranks, would come to the door, seeking a false friend, but hardly at this hour, and they were usually courteous. Hullo? she said again, and was beginning to think the sound of the buzzer was still part of her dream when she heard screaming.

Edith felt sure it was a woman's voice, though the entry system garbled sounds slightly, distorting speech. She felt sure she heard a young woman pleading to be let in, there was no mistaking the panic, she was saying she had been attacked, had run. Throwing caution to the wind, for she had heard appalling stories of city dwellers ignoring the helpless pleas of a murder victim, turning a deaf ear, a blind eye to killing, assault and robbery, Edith set her front door on the latch and hurried down the unlit staircase, still in only nightgown and slippers. The thought of a lonely young woman running for her life through deserted night streets was horrifying, this neighbourhood was known to be dangerous after dark. If it was foolish to be out at this hour, she had seen the young girls with nowhere to go, sleeping in doorways, haunting the underground station.

Edith had almost reached the ground floor when the animal leapt at her without warning. She had heard no sound, but suddenly claws were tearing her shoulders, hot breath scorching her throat. Its weight threw her to the ground, she found herself rolling, trying to shield her most vulnerable points, protect face and neck with her arms, kicking out blindly whenever she could, gasping for breath, but not finding enough of it to cry out.

She was curling up like a hedgehog, but without prickles, feeling his weight on her, the rapacious claws puncturing skin, his hot wet muzzle snapping and the growling sound issuing intermittently from the black bulk as his jaws went on snapping, ripping, searching for her jugular, the soft skin of her throat. She knew she could not drag herself back up two flights of stairs, the creature would not let her go, her dwelling might be in the sky, at this moment, for all the good it could do her. But in the midst of her frantic fight, struggling to survive, she had an inkling that the animal was playing cat and mouse with her, had no intention of killing her, for it could have done so within seconds. No, instinct told her he was letting go for a moment, easing off, only to see what she would do, then mauling her afresh, but not seriously enough to finish it.

Edith began inching her way towards the front door, felt the bristling doormat on her raw skin, its dust in her nostrils. Lying inert, the beast began sniffing idly at her bare legs. Then she suddenly stood upright, clutching at the wood surrounding the frosted glass to pull herself on to her feet, and twisted the nob of the lock. Quickly she opened the front door, just a fraction, just enough to slip out, then slammed it shut behind her.

Young Chris found her in the grey light of morning, huddled on the front steps. Her flesh was grey too, half frozen into immobility with cold. At first he could hardly get a word out of her, rubbing her icy skin, trying to get her indoors. Blood had dried on a myriad flesh wounds, and there was heavy bruising round her face and shoulders. He fetched his mother and together they got her back upstairs, wrapped in a blanket, step by stumbling step. Her raw nakedness was pathetic under the torn nightgown, and Chris willingly went to the kitchen whilst his mother put Edith to bed, first cleaning up her wounds. They found hot water bottles, and sent for the doctor. Jane attempted to get a cup of hot tea down her, holding the cup because Edith's hands were shaking so much, and bit by bit, through chattering teeth and livid lips, got the truth out of her. After which she rang the police.

. 14 .

The doctor prescribed a mild sedative and gave Edith a tetanus shot. He advised warmth, bed rest, and plenty of hot soup. Jane had rung the school to say she could not come in, sent Chris to get the prescription made up, and spent her time wandering in and out of Edith's bedroom, bringing cups of tea, or perching on the edge of the bed to chat reassuringly, hold her torn fingers soothingly between hers, or plump her pillows. She had also, very gently, brushed and combed her wildly dishevelled grey locks.

The police, when they finally arrived, were not helpful. They took their time, for a start. After terrifying the neighbourhood for so long with their screeching sirens, heedlessly scattering everybody in their path as they sped up the wrong side of the road, mounting pavements, ignoring traffic lights, the tenants had expected a prompt response, with several officers turning up on the doorstep almost immediately. But two hours after Jane had first rung the station she was still waiting impatiently, glancing out of a front window with increasing frequency for a sign of them.

Finally, towards noon, she saw a very youthful, fresh-faced constable who might, she thought, have been going to school with her own boy, strolling down the road in a leisurely sort of way. He paused outside the house, took a notebook from his breast pocket, apparently to check the address, and went up the path.

The boy, for Jane could only think of him as such, despite the uniform, did not seem to know why he had come, or what he should do. In every sense, he seemed utterly unequipped to deal with an emergency of any sort. Unarmed, he looked at her with innocent, disarming blue eyes and said he had been sent to investigate a burglary.

We could all have been murdered in our beds by now.

Jane felt disbelief mingling with rising exasperation. This was the result of ringing the emergency number hours ago.

The body is in the front room, with an axe through his skull.

The scared youth did not hear the edge of sarcasm in her voice. His Adam's apple went up and down within the stiff collar, too big for his tender neck. Jane took pity on him, seeing the terror in his clear blue eyes. It was not his fault if he had been sent, if the system did not function as it should. He was only a raw recruit, with the saving grace that he had not yet learnt to bully his way out of each and every blunder inflicted on the helpless community he was employed to serve.

It's not quite so awful, she said kindly, though goodness knows it's bad enough. And she told him what had

117

occurred during the night, though she had already given the story when she rang up. So you see, something has to be done about it, and done now. He has no business here, neither the dog nor his owner. Even if he were rightfully here, this is obviously wilful assault. The dog should be put down, removed immediately, and charges brought against his owner. Every tenant in this building is seriously at risk. Luckily we are not dealing with manslaughter. And it is by no means the first incident to frighten us.

By now she was speaking with severity, but a tremor shook her last words. The young boy was fiddling with his stiff new cap, shifting from foot to foot. The buttons on his brand new uniform were shining brightly.

If you wish to speak to the victim, by all means do. But I warn you, she is under sedation, doctor's orders, and I don't want her upset any further.

Jane opened the bedroom door and the young officer went awkardly through it, trying not to look to left or right, as if the exposure of under-garments, the intrusion into such chaotic, shabby indecency was painful to him. But the sight of Edith's discoloured, disfigured features was no less difficult for him. He kept looking at his notebook, glancing over his left shoulder, then his right, for a seat. Jane pushed an upright chair forward.

The young man cleared his throat.

I understand you wish to file a complaint.

She was pleading for help. What could I do?

Edith was slurring her words, her head tossing restlessly from side to side. The flesh round her eyes was now so puffy, she must have had difficulty in seeing.

What does she mean?

The young officer was not sure he had heard correctly. He was beginning to think the old woman was demented. He glanced round at her neighbour, who was not yet old and seemed to be in her right mind.

I'll tell you afterwards. Jane's voice was scarcely above a whisper. I don't want her put through too much now. She needs to sleep.

Looking puzzled, the young officer ran his fingers through his cropped hair, fair and stubbly. He coughed, twirling his short pencil.

When did this alleged attack occur?

Perhaps he was trying to stick to the rule book, having only recently learnt how to conduct an inquiry. But he was obviously struck by the absurdity of his own words.

Edith was trying to pull herself upright in bed, with difficulty, as though struggling with an unseen weight pressing down on her.

In the night. I was fast asleep. The doorbell woke me up. What is he doing in this house anyway? He is evil, wicked, I went right up to his door and asked him, downright rude to me. As for the dog, not permitted here, never been allowed. But she was pleading with me, a woman's voice, I was sure I heard a woman, really frightened.

Edith was becoming agitated at this memory, her damaged hands struggling with the bedclothes.

So you admitted a total stranger? In the middle of the night? The officer felt he was now on sure ground. Haven't you studied our leaflet, warning you of just this kind of thing? You must be on your guard. Never answer your door unless you know who it is. Such people will hoodwink you for your pension, a few quid, your bits and bobs.

But Edith could not hear him. The doctor's sedative had taken effect, and she slept.

Edith spent several days in bed, with Jane ensuring she was all right, popping in early each morning and again when she got back from school. She saw to it that Edith had hot food and did not get up too soon. After a few days, when the wounds had begun to heal, she ran a hot bath and helped her into it, pretending not to be aware of Edith's shame at such helplessness, at exposing her ugly old body. Unaware of Edith's embarrassment at such unexpected tenderness.

After the first shock, the extreme fatigue resulting from it, Edith was highly anxious about the situation which had brought her to this. For the moment she did not need to go out, but nevertheless she felt besieged, frightened. Whenever Jane came up she was terrified on her behalf, pleaded with her not to take any risks, and only the pills kept her fairly quiet. Her neighbour saw to it that she kept on taking them until she was more herself.

Jane, coming up with hot pies or vegetable soup, saw no sign of the dog. Nor did she hear him barking during the night. Although this made her task easier, it was also frustrating. She was determined to pursue the matter with the police, but this was difficult to do when the brute had apparently vanished into thin air. She had contacted the police several times, and on one occasion a senior police officer, together with a woman police constable, did visit the building at her request. But when neither dog nor his owner could be found, their manner became decidedly brusque and they came close to telling her that she was wasting police time, an offence for which she might be charged.

The flesh wounds no longer hurt, hard scabs peeling bit by bit, and the bruising turned various bright, livid colours before dying slowly as Edith began to return to a semblance of normality, pottering from room to room. She knew she could not stay indoors for ever, but her dread of venturing beyond her own front door was now so crippling, she almost welcomed continuing symptoms of her body's frailty and, as the bruising on her face faded to curious tints of green and yellow, declined to confront the world with such disfiguring marks. Her hip was stiff, her back hurt. She was not hungry anyhow.

The doctor paid a cursory visit and told her she could go out now, the fresh air would do her good. Exercise would get rid of the stiffness. Edith said nothing, but continued to put off the evil hour. So far she had not run out of excuses. Edith saw rainclouds gathering beyond the window, her back was bad, she had mislaid her keys, somebody might call.

It was whilst she was still convalescing that she got an unexpected visit from her brother and his wife. Edith had not spoken to either Robert or Marilyn in months, and for a fleeting moment she imagined a neighbour had informed them of her plight, and that they were concerned for her wellbeing. But, judging by their offhand manner and the fact that neither of them seemed to see anything odd about her looks, the horrid blemishes on her skin, her haphazard clothing and slow, shaky movements, they knew nothing and cared even less.

But then, both of them had always expected Edith to

look awful, and avoided looking at her directly. For Robert she was merely his sister who, so very unlike his wife, had never aspired to make something of herself. Marilyn went to an expensive hairdresser, who piled her carefully tinted locks in an eye-catching coiffure whilst an attendant manicurist painted her long nails bright red, a shade exactly matching her mouth. She wore expensive, colourful clothes adorned with a lot of brassy chains and buttons, as if designed to make them look cheap, and moved in a cloud of opulent perfume too heavy for her thin figure, such sharp features and scrawny limbs.

After the most cursory greeting, leaving her husband to do the small talk with Edith in the living room, Marilyn went off, from room to room, opening drawers, peering into cupboards, turning bits of furniture to the light, handling items standing about. Only after this had been going on for about fifteen minutes, with Marilyn calling out to her husband or occasionally popping her head round the door to enquire the whereabouts of a specific object, did it occur to Edith that her brother and his wife had come, after all these months, not to see her, but to find old Mrs Johnson's possessions. Edith heard Marilyn riffling through her mother's wardrobe, pushing coat-hangers along the rail, though what she expected to find amongst such dowdy, worn clothing Edith simply could not think.

Robert had been wandering about the room, apparently bereft of words, anything to say. He glanced out of the window, idly poked a finger into the rotting window frame, peered at the cracking plaster of walls and ceiling. Now, standing in the centre of the living room, he lit a cigarette and asked his sister for a drink.

Edith, who only kept sherry, obligingly poured him a glass of the dark amber liquid. It was sweet sherry. It struck her that this man, her brother, was not really interested in her presence, but had an obsessive curiosity about the fabric of the building in which she lived. He was now testing the floorboards, jiggling up and down on his highly polished shoes. Now he knelt down and started to tap at the skirting board, his sherry glass on the carpet. For a wild, fanciful moment Edith harboured the notion that Robert could be the unknown landlord. She knew he could be devious, but how far would he ultimately go? Would he resort to violence if necessary? Edith quickly suppressed such suspicions as unworthy of her, if not of him.

Robert's wife stood in the doorway, holding a rather ugly vase they had once presented to Mrs Johnson on her birthday. Not the last birthday, or even the one before that, but Marilyn never forgot a gift she had paid for. Now she was undecided whether to take it back. They had plenty of vases, it was the wrong colour, but it might do for those occasions, receptions, a sudden illness, when there were never enough of them in the house. She glanced towards her husband for a yes or no, but did not think to ask Edith whether she had any use for it, if she might take it. A moment later she was asking her the whereabouts of the diamond ring her mother-in-law had always intended to give her. She had been so touched by Mrs Johnson's sentiment, knowing what the ring meant to her, though of course the value was negligible, and she could hardly wear it without first getting it cleaned and perhaps reset, the setting being hopelessly ugly and old-fashioned. Nevertheless she might wear it now and then, just as a keepsake.

She gave Edith a kindly smile, as though conscious of doing her a favour.

But her expression rapidly clouded when Edith informed her that the ring had been sold off long ago, so long ago that it took her a moment to remember the item to which she was referring. A flicker of disbelief passing like a shadow over her brightly powdered face darkened to outright suspicion, suddenly aged the garish features, as Edith had seen rocky uplands turn unfriendly the moment clouds passed over the sun. She knew she had to justify herself. She also knew that if Marilyn got in this mood her only means of self-defence was attack.

It was her idea, not mine. Her dentures were hurting, paying for new ones cost far too much, we couldn't possibly afford it. I don't think she got much for it anyhow, not enough to pay for her new teeth, so you needn't fret.

I'm not fretting. Marilyn's voice was shrill, and she kept glancing across at Robert for support. He was now drinking up his sherry, wincing with disgust.

How much she got for it is hardly the point. No doubt the silly old woman sold it for a fraction of its real worth.

So it is the point. Edith found she was beginning to enjoy this argument. She saw her sister-in-law on the verge of losing control, and Robert was not helping.

Besides, I thought all that kind of thing, teeth and whatever, was free if you couldn't afford it.

You must be joking. When did you ever bother to find out what was going on?

How dare you speak to me like that! Marilyn was teetering dangerously on her high heels, and genuine blood rose under the makeup. Robert, speak to your sister!

But Robert was examining a chair in the corner of the room. Edith knew he could not stand Marilyn getting bitchy, losing her temper. He withdrew.

Calm down, both of you. If it's gone, it's gone, and that's all there is to it. You've got plenty of rings.

Edith, watching Marilyn's fingers flash as she tossed the vase angrily from left hand to right, had been thinking just this. Conspicuous stones vied with her bloodred fingernails for attention.

But I think we could use this oak chair. Not that it's worth much. But I remember it from my childhood, and it could go in our kitchen.

Edith knew that, if her brother said the chair was not worth much, then it had to be worth a bit, perhaps quite a bit. Robert was no connoisseur, but with a lifetime of wheeling and dealing behind him, he had an eye for anything saleable.

Edith felt the blood rush to her head, and old bruises beginning to hurt afresh. Not that Robert had so much as commented on the marks disfiguring her face, let alone expressed his concern. As usual, he saw only things, and everything he saw had a price to it. She felt her heart beginning to beat with painful rapidity, and could not control her feelings. After forfeiting her mother's house, why make a fuss about an old oak chair?

But Edith did make a fuss, and found she was making it, not so much on her own, but on old Mrs Johnson's behalf. Their mother had been silly, unkind, blind to Robert's defects, but she should not have been neglected. This was their first visit in nearly a year, and the money that should have been spent on their mother's comfort had not been spent. Edith had slaved her guts out to do what she could, but she could not afford much. Just remembering how her mother could not chew her food, her gums red-raw from ill-fitting dentures, was enough now. And her nerves were still edgy from the recent ordeal.

I want you both to go, she said firmly, speaking loudly enough to brook of no misunderstanding. The chair, for what it's worth, is staying here. So is that hideous vase you bought, though I can't stand the sight of it and I know you bought it cheap. Still, mother liked it. She was always a sucker for Robert. Put it down, Marilyn, and mind you don't break it.

Her sister-in-law let her jaw drop, seemed about to speak, but apparently thought better of it. Or perhaps could not think of anything. After a brief, uneasy silence she put down the vase.

You're not well. Marilyn spoke soothingly.

So you've finally noticed.

Robert's facial expression suggested that the volatility of women was beyond him.

Time to push off, he said shortly, and took his wife firmly by the elbow. There was no leave-taking.

· 15 ·

After their departure Edith noticed the small white card lying on the mantelpiece. She had been meaning to tell her brother about it, he had a right to know, but their behaviour had put everything else out of her mind. Not that she truly believed her father, their father, was alive after all these years, and that their childhood had been spent under a misconception. If it were so, it meant that, far from being a hero, he was a thoroughly bad lot, to say nothing of the light it cast on their mother. She had no wish to inflict all this on Robert, even if he deserved a shock, even if the story might go some way to explaining the way he had turned out. Perhaps he just had bad genes. No, she was being unkind. But she did feel he ought to be told, even if it was just a bureaucratic mix-up. And it would have been helpful for her, too, to discuss the matter openly and dispassionately. Whether she could ever have done so with Robert, was another matter. She had a deep, instinctive feeling that he would react badly to the news.

Simmering fury shook off the remnants of her lassitude. She picked up the white card, driven by sudden curiosity, but also a rather more mischievous emotion. In her resentment she was beginning to feel that she might have something on Robert, if there was even an inkling of truth in what Mr Reginald Ball (she read his name from the card) had told her. And she did wish to inflict it on him, upset his maddening equilibrium, throw him off balance. Moreover, if there was any question of either of them having to take any kind of responsibility for this no doubt dreadful old man, she would ensure that this time he, and only he, took it.

Edith began to dial the number printed on the card. She would tell this Mr Ball to get in touch with her brother, helpfully providing his home address. Even if the man was an outright impostor, not simply the victim of senility or bureaucratic bungling, it would set the cat amongst the pigeons. The fur would fly. Marilyn would lose her cool, they would possibly fight like cat and dog. Edith knew her sister-in-law when the claws were out.

The number kept ringing, but no reply. Edith's high spirits began to flag, dwindling into despondency. When she did get through, after several attempts, the extension number she had been given did not answer. She saw it ringing in an empty room. The switchboard operator intervened.

No reply, caller. Will you try later?

Edith sighed, feeling her momentum ebbing.

I'm trying to reach Mr Reginald Ball. Can I leave a message?

A brief silence, then: We have no Mr Ball at this building.

But I've seen him. He came to see me. I'm holding his card now.

There is nobody of that name on our list. What was it in connection with? Perhaps I could put you in touch with someone else.

My father. This Mr Ball said my father was in a home.

That would be Mr Willis, or Mr Kemp. I could try putting you through to one of them. Which home is he in?

I don't know. In any case, he's not my father. I'm sure of it. My father was killed in the war. Missing half a century ago, presumed killed.

There was a long, rather eerie silence.

Hullo? Edith thought she might have been accidentally disconnected.

Try the War Office, madam.

The operator spoke sharply, and now she was disconnected.

Edith sat by the silent telephone for what seemed like ages, but was probably only a few minutes. She felt foolish, and slightly out of control. If it had not been for Robert and that dreadful woman, coming here and upsetting her, it would never have occurred to her to follow the thing up. Clearly she had been the victim of a deception. Perhaps she was lucky to have got off so lightly. She told herself this, but felt no relief, only a different anxiety. She had heard of impostors performing operations in hospital and, although the patients survived, it was a disturbing thought. She did not know which was the more disturbing thought, the fact that a man could get away with it, and do the job, or that the victims could survive, apparently unscathed. Edith knew her mind was wandering, but could not think straight. If the card in her hand was solid, and it was, then she did not know where to begin.

But her wild and aimless musing on the meaning of the visiting card was, perhaps luckily, interrupted by unexpected and inexplicable sounds coming from down below, loud thuds and thumps echoing up the stairwell. In a house normally as still as this, any noises tended to command attention, however muted, but the racket going on below was not discreet.

Edith cautiously opened her front door, just far enough to peer out, but saw nothing. Leaning over the bannister she could see a ladder, several planks, and a zinc bucket at the bottom of the stairwell. Startled, Edith shut the door and went to a front window. A builder's lorry was parked just outside, and two men were unloading a second ladder from the back.

Edith was by turns bewildered, puzzled, hopeful. She did not know what to think. As far as she knew, nobody was planning to start redecorating. In the past there was usually some kind of warning, but she had heard nothing, and nowadays the tenants were too old to bother much. Even Mrs Gardiner, in former days such a stickler for decor, was now content to do nothing, to let things be, the wallpaper slowly fading, dust gathering on the ceiling. Nobody could stand the thought of so much upheaval, preferring rooms to stay as they had been for years now, imperceptibly growing old as they were doing. No, if major work was going ahead, it had to be the landlord setting things in motion.

A surge of sudden optimism lifted Edith's spirit. A new landlord, a new broom. She had been wrong to expect the worst from a change of ownership. She put her front door on the latch and crept cautiously down to the first landing, peering over the bannister as she went. Grey dust was rising up the stairwell, settling on the dark polish of the handrail, clouding the light from the high window, tickling in her nostrils. Down below she saw grey sheeting covering the old hall carpet, unevenly lapping the foot of the staircase.

What to do now? She could hear the two men talking, calling out to each other as they went to and fro, confidently moving about as if utterly unconcerned as to the presence or absence of residents in the building. They were crashing things heedlessly, laughing out loud at some shared joke. Neither of them glanced up as Edith came down the last flight of stairs. She felt as though she was shrinking.

Excuse me . . .

Edith had no wish to be seen as a nosy old busybody, but she did have a right to be seen. Neither of them had so much as turned round.

Excuse me . . .

So I said to 'er, I said, if it's fun yer looking for you've come to the right place.

The bigger of the two was speaking. He lit a cigarette and flung the used match on the floor, now almost impassable with planking, tools, and loosely spread sheeting. Edith saw a blue snake tattooed on his muscular bare arm.

Should have seen the size of 'er. Melons out front to sink yer teeth into, and two more rahnd the back to grab on ter.

He began to laugh, billowing smoke, then coughing. The smaller of the two was kicking idly at a sack of plaster, sending up a cloud of dry white dust. Edith found herself sneezing violently, and both men turned to look at her.

Would you mind telling me what is going on?

She spoke firmly, stepping down to their level. The smaller of the two had a squint, and was now leering at her, revealing black gaps between brown teeth.

What does it look like?

He cocked one eyebrow at her, lifting it with contempt.

I'm asking you.

Edith's voice shook slightly at this impudence, but she had no intention of being put off. The big fellow went casually to the window, pushed it open and flung out his cigarette stub.

Look lady, we got our orders. He spoke brusquely. You mind your business, we'll mind ours. All right?

And with this the two men went through the street door, slamming it hard behind them. Through the open window Edith saw them stroll down the path, get into the cab of their lorry, drive off. Cold air was blowing in, and she stepped gingerly over the mess to shut it.

She heard the door behind her open. Mrs Gardiner, her face ashen, was peering out, her safety chain still slung across.

Who are they? she demanded, her voice scarcely above a whisper. What's going on?

I never found out.

Edith's mood had sunk into despondency. The brief excitement of the moment had fizzled out, and with it all sparks of optimism. Whatever was happening, or about to, was beyond her control. It might be good or bad, or nothing. She only knew that each hour seemed to bring its own disorder, something unexpected. This she now had to expect, which was no comfort.

But Mrs Gardiner was watching her with frightened, childish eyes.

Oh Edith.

It was a cry from the heart, for Mrs Gardiner had not addressed her by her first name in thirty years. The proud, imperious old bitch had begun to crumble, visibly, like a stately home when the roof falls in. She was a pitiful wreck of her former self. Edith took pity on her.

She had no wish to sit with her, listening yet again to a litany of the fears and fantasies which had begun to haunt her, but she went in when Mrs Gardiner took off the safety chain, pleading with her to come inside, if only for a moment.

Mrs Gardiner's terror of the leather-clad thug and his dog, even though both had been lying low, had been augmented by the attack on Edith. Stillness and invisibility did nothing to diminish it, on the contrary, her imagination now fed on the unknown, on constant uncertainty. She was refusing to answer her doorbell, even in broad daylight, even when she was expecting a grocery delivery. She got Chris or Edith to bring in parcels left on the doorstep for her. Edith frequently found herself having to pay off a butcher bringing two lamb chops, or let in the driver of her laundry service. Mrs Gardiner had also begun watching nervously from behind her net curtains for suspicious signs, a man apparently skulking round the back, a light flashing after dark in the trees, and would call up her neighbours in great agitation.

What is going on?

Mrs Gardiner was still speaking in a whisper, clutching

at Edith's wrist. She had begun to shrink, had lost her dignified bearing. Now her fading eyes were on a level with Edith's.

I don't know. Must be the landlord, whoever he is.

Edith tried to sound cheerful. It was only by reassuring Mrs Gardiner that she could hope to escape from her clinging insecurity. She might have found her previous behaviour obnoxious, but it was less of a burden.

I must go, she said, but without much conviction. There was something odd about her neighbour's hallway, she thought, noticing a discoloration on the fading, dusty wallpaper, an oval patch on the regency pattern. Then she remembered there had been an antique gilt mirror where the lighter colour now stood out, a ring of dark dust round it. Her eye began wandering, beyond Mrs Gardiner's woolclad form. A slender side table of inlaid mahogany had also gone missing, together with the set of silver-backed brushes which stood on it.

Mrs Gardiner was now dragging her into the front room, clutching her walking stick in her other hand. The room was in semi-darkness, the heavy curtains half drawn across the big bay window.

Do you think he is a burglar?

Who?

Mrs Gardiner lifted her stick, pointing at the far wall dividing her flat from the other ground floor apartment.

I shouldn't think so, Edith retorted drily. Burglars don't normally move in.

But she did not go on to articulate her own anxiety, knowing that her neighbour was too fragile to hear it. Through the shadowy light she saw the room now had a curious nakedness about it. Shelves bare of their usual ornaments, pictures missing, fewer chairs. And the carpet looking unexpectedly worn and threadbare with use.

. 16 .

Edith took her first outing the following morning. Only to the local shops, but it was a start. She felt a little uncertain on her legs. Also, it seemed to her that the sounds of traffic were abnormally loud, giving her an odd sensation of vertigo. She could not tell just where sounds were coming from, which made her feel slightly dizzy, and just a bit frightened of getting run over. She knew that ears were as important as eyes in getting across roads safely, and that it might well be defective hearing which cost the elderly their lives.

When she got back she had to step over the clutter left by the workmen. There had been no sign of them today. The stuff lying about was a nuisance: the dusty sheeting had not been spread smoothly, it lay in deceiving folds and bumps, which could catch your heels; planks, buckets and other tools had been left here, there and everywhere, some of it hidden from the unwary by uneven sheeting.

The workmen did not return the following day either.

After a fortnight the tenants had almost got used to living with the mess. Bit by bit items were moved out of harm's way, closer to the walls. Chris came in after school to help shift the heaviest equipment. Together with Edith he straightened the sheeting, so that nobody could catch their heels in its folds, risking an accident. Mrs Gardiner, leaning on her walking stick, stood by her front door, watching. She might have been the first to fall, now that her gait was so uncertain. Chris put the ladders behind the front door, in an alcove, then began lifting a stack of planks. Mrs Gardiner told him he was a good boy, and Edith saw him flush dark crimson, though perhaps only from exertion. Then, leaning heavily on her stick, the old woman limped indoors, telling him not to go away, and brought back an apple, which she pressed into his hand. Chris, looking awkward, had the courtesy to accept it. A child of grace, thought Edith proudly, smiling slily, where neither of them could see her.

Edith was having one of her bad dreams. Her brother Robert and a grotesque old man whom she had never seen in her waking hours but knew, in the way such things are known in dreams, was her father, were chiselling into the brickwork of her bedroom, creating jagged gaps in the walls through which she could clearly see grey daylight. She woke suddenly and heard actual sounds coming from beyond her front door, a loud hammering echoing up the stairwell. It was still early. She drew back the bedroom curtain and saw a dull dawn, then hastily put on dressing gown and slippers.

The lorry was parked outside, and on her landing the two men were working at the high window. The bigger fellow with the brawny arms was perched on top of a ladder, banging a chisel into the window frame, whilst his mate held the ladder steady. He had a cigarette dangling from the corner of his mouth, the ash dropping down his paint-smeared overalls.

What are you doing?

Edith had to step down to their level and repeat the question before either of them appeared to hear her.

The wood's rotten, muttered the smaller of the two, squinting at her through a column of smoke. He dug a dirty thumbnail into the woodwork. Like mouldy cheese, he added, whilst the man on the ladder went on banging. Bits of wood were falling to the floor.

So?

This was hardly news to Edith. The windows had been rotten for years.

So they've got to go.

He ground his cigarette stub into the window sill and spat.

I'm glad to hear it.

Edith was agreeably surprised to find such consensus. Things were looking up. She had been wrong to be suspicious, distrustful, and most certainly should not have got despondent. Patience was required, the long view. She went indoors, put the kettle on, humming to herself. She offered mugs of tea to the two workmen, who thanked her enthusiastically.

The noise continued through the morning. The two men, having removed the tall leaded window on the second floor landing, started work on the floor below. Edith was sad to see the windows go, even if they were rotten. The tiny leaded panes had style, and she suspected that whatever was put in their place would not be nearly as appropriate, perhaps rather ugly. Still, it was necessary to make the house weatherproof, and it was too much to expect the owner to go to the expense of reproducing them. Cold air was now blowing through the gap, rattling her front door. By mid-morning it had begun to rain, windy squalls which blew into the unprotected stairwell, soaking the old wallpaper and carpet.

The men left at noon, and Edith saw them load the old windows into the back of the lorry. Then they drove off. It was annoying that they should have gone, no doubt for lunch, without first putting up some protective sheeting, but perhaps they had driven off to collect new windows, making such precautions almost superfluous. Even the best workmen could be a bit slapdash, it went with the job.

The sky was still dark. It stopped raining, then began again. Two hours went by, but no sign of the men. Edith kept looking out of her windows, but saw only unknown cars, unknown persons passing, hurrying under black umbrellas. Anxious now, she could not bring herself to turn away from the window, focus her mind on other things, get on with living as best she could. Any sense of outrage was numbed by bleakness and cold.

Night had begun to fall, early now, with winter coming. Tyres swishing in water, and car lights dazzling on falling rain. Through the wind, draughts rattling doors and windows, she heard, faintly, Mrs Gardiner calling out from below. If she had not been sitting, watching barren trees thrashing across the garish aura of street lamps, she might not have heard her.

Cold wind blew through her clothing as she hurried down. The lights were not working, and she had to step cautiously over the wreckage in the moving shadows. The stairwell was surreal, ghostly, the product of a dream, or of a war, and Mrs Gardiner, too, appeared like a ghost, grey hair and pallid features eerily lit from the street, windblown, forlorn. Edith saw two tears glistening down her frightened face.

Get inside, you'll catch your death.

Edith led her through her own front door. Limping, leaning heavily on her stick, Mrs Gardiner went with the docility of a sick child. Edith took her through to the living room, now lit only from the street, and set her down on the sofa. Then she saw that, apart from the sofa, the room was quite empty. There was bare shelving along the wall opposite, otherwise nothing.

· 17 ·

Edith slept fitfully, strong winds waking her at intervals.
She could feel the bed swaying with the house, and heard
dustbin lids rattling below. In the grey morning light she
saw the trees tossing and whirling in the mocking wind.
Cold air blew under her front door, chilling her ankles,
biting through to the bone. She could not keep doors
firmly shut, they just went on slamming to and fro, a
maddening sound. When she attempted to open her front
door she was struck by the full force of the wind. It threw
her backwards, sending bills and letters flying, knocking a
pot plant to the floor. The stairwell had the air of an
abandoned shipwreck: a lot of water had blown in
overnight, also bits of rubbish and soggy leaves.

It took all her strength to get the door shut, and
afterwards she was shivering helplessly. Everything about
her felt damp. Teeth chattering, she tried to catch some
warmth from the simmering kettle. Through the kitchen
window skeletal trees went on with their macabre dance,

writing and twisting in the wind. No sign of the workmen, or their lorry. By now she felt too ill to worry, beyond either expecting or hoping. She went back to bed.

During the following hours Edith lost all sense of time. The wind was still buffeting the house, rattling the sash window, slamming doors. She dozed off and found an old man sitting on the edge of her bed, smiling at her as though she was a child. She knew this, she was now a child, because he was leaning forward, swinging an old fob-watch on a gold chain. Blow, he told her, and when she did so its lid flew open, and she saw the gothic numbers and two hands pointing. She knew this trick had been played on her before, her grandfather did it. Somewhere there was a hidden spring which made the watch open, only she did not know where it was. She felt breathless.

This confusion between past and present, cause and effect, far from disturbing her, was oddly reassuring. She felt weightless, light as a feather, drifting between dream and reality. Even the steady drip from her leaking ceiling did not worry her. She kept her eyes closed, saw rings gently running in concentric circles on the smooth surface of a millpond. Nothing could disturb the underlying serenity of her position. If there was a God somewhere, then he held her. If not, then letting go was not too difficult either.

The day was almost over when she woke up, dusk falling and shadows gathering in the corners of the room. She heard the distant sound of homeward traffic but closer, coming from the floor below, thin lucid music. Listening to the unearthly melody, she also heard rooks cry harshly in the high trees. She was content to go on lying, to do nothing.

Edith? Are you all right?

It was Jane calling, so she got up. Feeling weak in head and legs, the world swayed slightly. It was as though she was walking the deck of a ship on the high seas. Opening her front door, a blast of cold air entered with her friend. Even though it was too dark to see much, Edith could smell the foul weather which had soaked into the building's fabric, an odour of decay emanating from everything, wood, paper and plaster, even brickwork. She lacked the strength to shut the door on her own.

The two women went into the cold living room. Jane lit the lamps, drew curtains, but the chill in the room would not go. Edith had sunk into a chair, her head swimming. Jane took a closer look at her, touching her forehead.

You're feverish. This can't go on. This house will be the death of you. It's the weekend. Tomorrow I'll buy some plastic sheeting. Chris can help put it up. And next week I will try to find out just what is going on here, and get it put right. This is simply outrageous.

Under the lamplight Edith saw features haggard with fatigue. To Edith she was still young and, as usual, she spoke now with the fiery passion which social injustice roused in her. But she had a physique that would not endure, in which early blossoming quickly turns to dust. Her fair hair had lost its lustre, hung limp, cut in a style too youthful. Her skin had lost its bloom, grown grey and porous, the features coarsening.

It's dangerous. Those windows are very high.

Edith felt the boy took too many risks. Ever since she

had known him, she had been worrying. When he began climbing trees, riding a bicycle.

Don't worry. I'll keep an eye on him.

Nevertheless, even as she told Edith not to worry, she was frowning, biting her fingernails. To Edith, she looked worn out. Edith thought she had too much responsibility, and now it was showing. When she first knew her Jane had been such a pretty woman, joyous too.

The roof is leaking. If you could tell them, my roof is leaking. What if my ceilings come down?

She had not meant to burden her further. Her friend had too much responsibility as it was. But the words kept tumbling out of her, from weakness, because she felt ill.

Her friend was guiding her back to the bedroom. She did not want Jane to see her like this, with helpless tears now running down her cheeks, but was powerless to prevent it.

Jane brought in a hot water bottle, tucking it under her bedclothes. Then she looked round the untidy bedroom, up at the damp ceiling, down at the pan half full of rainwater.

This is awful. Why don't you move into your mother's room for now?

No.

Edith's reply was unexpectedly brusque, giving way to a fit of coughing.

The coughing continued through the night. In the morning she got up and put on several layers of thick clothing. But everything felt damp. Her feet had swollen and she could not squeeze them into outdoor shoes. It had been a windy night, and the road was strewn with wet litter and branches broken from trees. Wet wallpaper was hanging loose in a corner of the stairwell, and water squelched from the carpet under her weight.

On the first floor landing Martha Wolf was picking up bits of litter blown in from the street, rubber gloves on her hands, a headscarf tied under her long chin. She was bent over like a ragpicker and, as if by common consent, the two women did not exchange a word. As if, by saying nothing, they might pretend that nothing was going on.

There were no letters for Edith, only bills for Mrs Gardiner. To prevent them from blowing away, Edith put them back in the mail basket.

When she went back, Martha Wolf was no longer on the stairs. Edith felt uneasy, climbing laboriously up to the second floor. Perhaps she should have spoken. Knowing, as she did, their background, perhaps it had been wrong of her to say nothing. Still, it was too late, she could hardly go down now and ring their doorbell. But she had not been to see Rhoda for far too long. Suddenly she felt bad about it, even if Rhoda's behaviour had been odd. Comparing her own conduct to that of Jane Lamb, she knew hers fell short.

As a peace offering, Edith took a small bottle of rum from the kitchen. This she had kept for her mother, who had a liking for a medicinal hot toddy now and then. Rhoda also enjoyed a dash of something strong in a hot drink if she had a cold, and even when she did not.

She heard footsteps coming down the narrow passage only moments after she had rung the bell. They were coming at a brisk tempo, which lifted Edith's spirit. Obviously Rhoda was her old self once more, and full of vigour. But the eyes looking into hers after the door had opened were not Rhoda's, and Edith found herself looking at a youngish woman she had never encountered before. This person had a resentful expression, as though she did not welcome callers. She stood blocking the doorway, legs apart, arm akimbo. She was frowning, and the two long earrings dangling from her pierced lobes were in the form of silver arrows. They shook slightly.

Yes?

She was uncompromisingly abrupt.

Edith found herself without words. In all the years she had been dropping in on her, Rhoda had never had visitors. If she had family, she had long lost touch, for she mentioned nobody. As for friends, she met them only on neutral ground, in drinking clubs, or on the organised outings and trips which she took on a regular basis. Within her own four walls she had lavished her intimacy only on Felix.

The person holding the door moved, as if about to shut it. Edith took a step forward and finally found her tongue.

I'm Rhoda's friend, she said firmly. I've come to see her.

Auntie is too sick to see anybody.

But this person was smiling, as if in triumph. A grin resembling nothing so much as a sneer.

She'll see me.

No.

Ask her.

Edith now felt an urgent wish to see Rhoda, if only because it was being denied her.

No. She's sleeping. I don't want to disturb her.

I've brought her this.

146

This person, who could not be Rhoda's niece, glanced down at the half bottle of rum. Her arm came out, quick as a lizard's tongue, to snatch it. Then she suddenly shut the door without saying a word.

. 18 .

Equipped with hardboard, hammer and nails, and a plentiful supply of plastic sheeting, Chris and a young schoolfriend came to block up the empty window frames. This created a bit of a stir, it was almost exciting. Tenants emerged from their individual doors to watch them working, offer helpful suggestions, perhaps lend a hand. Most surprisingly, even the Wolfs emerged from hiding. Martha brought out a box of chocolates for the boys, whilst Fred unexpectedly proved to be a handyman, skilfully sawing hardboard to fit the window gaps correctly.

For an hour or two the silent, crumbling old house rang to the sound of hammering, of words passing to and fro, even mirth. The boys nailed the hardboard across the lower two thirds of the window frames and, so the residents could see where they were going, plastic sheeting across the top. They stood precariously on ladders, hammering away, whilst Edith and Martha kept telling them not to fall.

It reminded Edith of her childhood during the war, when losing windows was a common occurrence, and grown-ups were in the habit of helping each other out, offering shelter and hot cups of tea, being friendly. Whether Martha Wolf was also reminded of those years, or not, after the work on the stairs was finished Edith was invited into the Wolfs' flat, ostensibly for tea.

This was so unexpected that Edith was taken aback, and found it hard to make small talk. So far she had never even stepped into their hallway, now she was led into a room that took her breath away. It was a library rather than a living room, with shelves all round, running from floor to ceiling. The books were old, with frayed spines, dark bindings in fading brown, maroon, with lettering in black or gold. There were books stacked in the corners of the room too, since the shelving was full, some with their spines missing, showing backing and old glue.

If Edith felt uncertain how to conduct herself, Martha also seemed unsure, nervously handling cups and saucers, doing things slightly wrong, pouring too much milk or too little, serving tea that was much too weak. She kept apologising, whilst Edith kept saying never mind, I really don't mind. But whilst she was sipping the milky tea Edith could hear stealthy footsteps in the neighbouring room, surreptitious movements. Fred Wolf did not come in to join them, nor did he appear in the hallway when Edith left.

Jane Lamb did seek legal advice, even though she was not directly threatened by recent events. As a result they were visited by an inspector equipped with clipboard and pen. He made a few notes, asking the tenants which

149

contractor was doing the work, or not doing it, but nobody could tell him, since the men had used an unmarked lorry. The inspector pointed out that it was not uncommon for such firms, particularly if they only had a few workmen, to work simultaneously on several jobs, though he agreed the situation was unsatisfactory.

He took a look at the damp patches on Edith's ceilings, stepping up on a chair to touch the soggy plaster after first placing two thick telephone directories on its seat so as to give himself more height, but found himself still too short. He told her it would be necessary for him to see the rain coming through, if he was to take action. Edith, who had spent hours trying to contact an official in his office, stared back at him in incredulity. She should, he said kindly, give him a ring during a rainstorm and he would come round. But, she stammered, it was so difficult to get through, and she had been told no inspector was available after eleven in the morning. He was smiling now: that's right, ring before eleven. So it must rain first thing in the morning? He nodded. And if it stops by the time you get here? But the inspector was now tapping a skirting board, and did not seem to be listening.

However, despite the seemingly hopeless nature of his task, the inspector conscientiously went on to look at the ancient window frames and sclerotic plumbing, pushing sashes, turning taps. He left Edith to visit other tenants, but afterwards returned to tell her of another problem. It was necessary for the council to gain access to every part of the building before taking legal action, and there seemed to be a problem with one of the ground floor flats. He had been told by a resident that this was presently occupied illegally, or by a henchman of the landlord. He had tried to gain entry, but there had been no reply. Obviously, he continued, the person at present occupying the premises is unlikely to give access voluntarily, and this would require separate legal action, or the threat of it, as a preliminary to all other proceedings.

I thought I had better warn you now. Before you get too hopeful.

Edith did not know whether to laugh or cry. She stood on her threshold, listening to his footsteps receding down the stairwell. Through the plastic sheeting covering the window she could see daylight, but only dimly, the sheeting being now thick with grime. It was cold comfort to be told all this would cost her nothing, the law was free, if it had already cost her too much, and was set in motion too tardily. On a bad night she did not know whether she could withstand another winter.

Her dreams were now more sombre. She thought she was creeping through a dank and muddy tunnel, without light, and with no end in sight.

. 19 .

The last of Mrs Gardiner's furniture was being taken away. Edith, looking down from her kitchen window early on Monday morning, saw two men in brown overalls carry a handsome wardrobe down the front steps. A few moments later they went back inside, returning with a matching dressing table. Clearly, Mrs Gardiner had had enough. It was hardly surprising, anybody who could afford to get out of this house, with conditions worsening day by day, would obviously do so.

Edith hurried downstairs to say goodbye to her old neighbour. Whatever their differences in the past, she now felt pity for her. Mrs Gardiner, perhaps on account of her age, possibly on account of the upbringing which had made her so insufferable, was now least able to cope with the changing situation in the house.

She found the front door ajar, heard the two men's voices echoing in the empty front room. Edith went through to the bedroom, seeing the open door. But instead of the crates and boxes she expected to find, saw an entirely different kind of mess. Heaps of clothing lay on the double bed, strewn on the floor too. Suits and silk dresses, still on their fancy hangers, a few zipped into protective covers. Lacy nightgowns, a welter of under-wear, and dozens of shoes covering the carpet. In the midst of this sat Mrs Gardiner, in a kind of frozen immobility.

She did not react to Edith's presence. She might have been deaf to it, blind, or merely indifferent. Edith's first thought was that senility had struck her, suddenly; her second, that she was simply too old, too set in her ways, to cope with this upheaval, and had given up. It was even possible she had got the date wrong, a mix-up which had left her unprepared. Hence her clothing strewn about, unpacked.

Can I do anything?

Edith touched her on the shoulder, but Mrs Gardiner did not react. Looking down at her, Edith could see, in her thinning hair, a small bald patch which was not normally visible. When she held herself erect Mrs Gardiner had more height than Edith. Now she was stooping forward, slumped on the edge of the bed.

She slowly shook her head, but seemed bereft of speech. Sinking on to the edge of the bed, Edith put an arm round her.

What is it?

Mrs Gardiner did not reply. She gave off an odour of stale perfume and powder. Edith was stroking the lambs-wool covering her shoulder.

What is it? she repeated. Shall I give you a hand with moving?

I'm not moving.

She was whispering, hardly audible, toying with her fingers.

But –

She suddenly squared her shoulders and went on, more loudly now.

My solicitor. Everything was left in trust. My husband thought it for the best. He did not want me to have the worry. Obviously I know nothing about such things. He took care of everything. And now it has all gone. Shares, annuities, everything. I don't understand it. He must have been cheating me for years. Such a nice man, I thought, and always so courteous. It never occurred to me, not till the regular payments stopped. And even then I thought the bank was in error. Well you would, wouldn't you? I was told he had left the country, for good apparently. Client's funds are missing. Seems he has been covering up for years.

Edith could not think of anything helpful to say. Mrs Gardiner was toying with the wedding ring on her left hand, twisting it between finger and thumb. The other rings had vanished.

They have to leave my bed, she went on, looking round the chaotic room. It's the law.

She spoke meekly, almost sounding childish, a small girl confessing to a distressing incident which she had not fully understood.

I'll help you to tidy up.

Edith got up and saw the two men, who had taken all they were permitted to confiscate, off the premises. She did what she could, whilst Mrs Gardiner continued to sit as though the bed were a raft in a stormy sea, and she had survived a shipwreck.

There was no hiding the vacuum, but Edith did what she could. She brought down a few bits of furniture which had belonged to her mother. They were old and shabby, and Edith was conscious how poor they must look to Mrs Gardiner, in comparison to what she had been used to. But at least the rooms did not look quite so empty, for the moment. What to do about Mrs Gardiner in the longer term, she knew, was a more difficult problem. Clearly she was helpless, in shock. Obviously she had nobody to rely on now or, if she did, had no idea how to turn to them at this moment. She thought she would try to find out, discreetly, the whereabouts of a son she thought must be somewhere in the world. And there was also a married daughter, though she had got the impression the two did not get on. Nevertheless, if the latter was living in this country, it was surely right, at such a juncture, for her to be discreetly informed.

Edith kept turning such thoughts over, wondering whether to discuss the problem with Jane Lamb, who was likely to know the best way to go about things. Edith was fearful of meddling, of upsetting the poor old woman further by prying, perhaps re-opening old wounds. Yes, there had been mention of a son working abroad, but it had been a long time ago, and Edith had no idea which continent it had been.

In the evening Edith tried to contact her friend in the basement, but nobody was in, apparently, and she saw no lights in any of the windows.

In the event the problem of Mrs Gardiner was solved, quickly and unexpectedly. By the following morning she had gone. Nobody had heard anything during the night,

155

and no forwarding address was left behind. A few days later her windows were boarded up, and Edith found her mother's bits of furniture lying near the dustbins.

. 20 .

The house now felt semi-deserted. It was eerily silent for most of the day, dark, windswept, as the tenants hid from the world. No guests arrived at the front door, no cheerful hubbub of ordinary living. And tenants had begun to leave garbage lying on their landings, not bothering to take it down to the dustbins. It had begun with Rhoda's niece, who was, Edith felt sure, no niece, but soon Edith found the weather too inclement, and took to leaving bags of rubbish outside her own front door rather than struggling up and down the dank staircase. The plastic sheeting had torn in a high wind, letting wind and water in, flapping noisily.

One wintry morning a lorry arrived, and several men began unloading scaffolding. But it was left lying at the side of the house, for days, indefinitely. Letters were left unclaimed in the hall, for Rhoda, Mrs Gardiner, and for persons who had never lived in the house. Edith did receive a notification from the local authority listing thirty-seven defects in the building which would require repair if and when the legal owner could be identified and charged. The ceiling in her bedroom collapsed and she moved, unwillingly, into her mother's bedroom.

The first Edith knew of the break-in down in the basement was when she heard sirens wailing through the dark. This was a normal background noise in the city nowadays and she only went to her window when the piercing noise unexpectedly stopped, not dying off gradually. Down below were two white vehicles, blue lights flashing, dark figures going to and fro between pavement and area steps.

When she got down to the basement, hurrying as fast as her feet would carry her, she saw Chris unconscious on the living room floor, dark blood matted down the side of his face and in his hair. Two men were attending to him, now lifting him very gently on to a stretcher. A woman put a transparent mask over his nose and mouth.

I don't know how long he's been like this, Jane was breathlessly answering an ambulance man. I only just got back. From rehearsing the school play. For the festive season.

Still in her outdoor coat, she was trying to help the men to negotiate the stretcher through the open door when she saw Edith. She spoke abruptly: Stay here. I'm going to the hospital.

His eyes were shut. They had put a red blanket over him. Edith stood, watching him being borne up the area steps. Jane, following behind, hurrying into the night. She heard the siren wailing shrilly through the dark, and in its dying wake saw, beyond the sulphureous light from the street, way above the naked trees, a black sky overhead. The air was dry and cold. A new moon had risen over the rooftops.

It was only after she had turned back from the door, shut it fast, that Edith saw the mess in the flat. Not a stick of furniture but had been broken, not a wall which had not been daubed with paint, or with matter which was dark, smelly, disgusting. Curtains had been torn from the windows, pot plants tipped over, cushions ripped. Scattered over the floors were books torn out of their bindings, the contents of cupboards, Chris's old toys. Bedding had been slashed and soiled, empty beer cans left strewn about. Shards of crockery lay on the kitchen floor in a pool of milk.

Edith did what she could, but her mind was not on it. Wandering aimlessly from room to room, she set a chair upright, put pot plants back on window sills, swept broken china into a dustpan. She could do nothing, she felt, about the bedding, and trying to put book pages back in their correct covers was utterly beyond her. A lamp lying on the living room floor was still lit, and she set it upright, cautiously. It was not much, the little she could do, and the immensity of the task, of putting things right, was beyond her. Nothing, she felt, could be put right. Not ever. Stupid with incomprehension, utterly at the end of her tether, Edith put her feet up on the despoiled sofa in the wreck of the living room. Thinking only of the boy, numb in mind and body, she kept looking at the mindless, wild graffitti all round her. Trying to read the unreadable, comprehend this foreign language. If she went on staring long enough, she felt, it might finally make some kind of sense. Towards dawn, with the lights still on in every room, she slept.

*

She was woken by the sound of a key turning in the lock, and Jane was standing over her, ashen of face, valleys of darkness under her eyes.

He's conscious. Thank God, he's conscious now. Badly concussed. Can't remember a thing. Doctors say he's badly concussed, too early to say if any lasting effect. Broken ribs, they think, but that's nothing. Sleeping now. The best for him.

She was going to sit down, absently, exhausted, still in her outdoor coat. Then she suddenly, as if seeing only now, took in the room, the mess it was in.

Oh my God.

Out of her a dry flat laugh, almost a cough.

I'm sorry about the mess.

Edith swung her feet to the floor. She was feeling very stiff.

You're sorry!

I did what I could, but . . .

Edith had run out of words.

She got up, still a bit numb, thinking she must make a cup of tea, even if the kitchen was in an unholy mess. Jane had clearly had a dreadful night, and was looking broken. She was slumping now, still in her outdoor clothes, at the end of the sofa.

I'm moving out, Edith. I've had it.

Edith forgot what she was intending to do, stood still.

This is no place to bring up a child. I've got to think of him.

Edith felt as if an essential fluid was rapidly draining out of her, robbing her of strength.

I'm sorry. I know I'm letting you down. But I have to

160

put Chris first. You would, in my position. I've been offered a job far away from this bloody city. I was in two minds about it, but not now. There's nothing left here, is there? Nothing worth fighting for.

She was looking round the ruined room, a picture hanging askew, its glass broken, bright cushions vomiting their innards, everything she had built up so lovingly, not with wealth, but a loving imagination. Edith had never seen her look so limp, so utterly bereft of spirit.

You'll feel better after a cup of tea.

But Edith knew she would not, as she stumbled round the devastated kitchen, trying to find a teapot which had not been smashed, unbroken cups, a drop of leftover milk not soiling the floor. Her hands were trembling, for she knew this spirit would not rekindle, and with it the guiding light, the most meaningful fire of her wintry days, had burnt out. As she brought the tea tray into the awful wreck of the living room she kept trying to think of words which might ameliorate the situation, encourage Jane to see things differently, to reconsider her decision. But she found nothing to say, or rather, could not utter the words which kept springing to her lips, longing to burst out: don't abandon me, please don't take him from me.

Edith did not see Chris, ever again. The attack had been too traumatic, and it was hardly worth trying to put the basement flat to rights for such a brief period. Packing a few essentials, Jane went to stay with a nearby friend, from where she took her son immediately to his new home.

. 21 .

Ferns frosted over the windows by morning. It was bitterly cold. Deceptively bright skies of opalescent light, frozen puddles, rime turning lawns whitish. Edith found it difficult to keep warm, put on several layers of woollen clothing when she got up, slept in thick socks and an old cardigan. Although it was so cold, and she dreaded the fuel bill, this crisp weather was oddly bracing, the wintry sunlight cheering. At least she did not need to worry about rain coming through her ceiling whilst the sky was so clear, without a cloud to be seen.

But after several days of high pressure a problem occurred. One evening, the water in her bath did not drain away after she had pulled the plug. She found it in the morning, cold and scummy. Martha came up to the second floor to report a similar situation in their flat, in fact dirty water from Edith's bath had run into theirs. Obviously the outflow pipe had frozen up, no doubt starting in the empty ground floor flat. A tap left dripping would have been enough, and now the ice was solid through the entire length of the pipe. Even if it were possible to break into the empty flat, even if they could find the means and the temerity to do it, this would not help. Both knew from past experience that no plumber, no blowtorch, would loosen the ice. Nothing would shift it until the temperature changed, and it thawed.

Day-to-day living was now even more strenuous, an uphill struggle. Every drop of water used, whether in bathroom or kitchen, had to be bailed laboriously into a bucket, then tipped down the lavatory. Edith knew this was not the worst: if other pipes had frozen there might have been no water. She tried to cut down the washing up, cooking simply, doing without. She stubbornly refused to give up her bath, and spent what seemed like hours getting rid of the water.

Edith was not now thinking of the future or, very much, of the past. There was no sign of the two workmen, or their lorry, but she had ceased to gaze out of the window, hoping for a glimpse of them. There was too much to do, and it was too tiring, to leave leisure for wishful thinking. She had given up expecting things to be put right, assuredly not here and now. As for tomorrow, it was too far off. Every minute of each hour was now fully utilised, with no energy left over for thought.

The Wolfs' water heater suddenly did not work, adding to the difficulty of washing up. Edith helped Martha to wash her hair even though it took hours, afterwards, to get rid of the suds. A new intimacy, shy at first, had begun to blossom between them. It had to, now that they took turns to bend over and rinse dirt and suds from each other's greying hair. Now that Martha was bringing up pans

163

which needed scouring, lending a hand with the task of bailing, mopping up puddles which inevitably spilled on the floors.

And Fred Wolf did his bit too. He decided the two women should be let off their labours, at least for a night, and insisted on taking them both to a local restaurant. Edith tried to smarten herself up a bit before they left the house, feeling nervous of this unexpected sociability. Fred took each woman by the elbow, guiding them almost briskly through the dark streets of the neighbourhood. He confined himself to the odd word, an exclamation now and then, just setting the pace, whilst Edith and Martha were huffing and puffing too much, in an effort to keep up with him, to talk.

Settled in the restaurant, however, gazing contently into the mellow glow of the candle flame softening their features, its light flickering from the centre of the tablecloth, the cosy atmosphere loosened their tongues, melted their inhibitions. The restaurant was empty, apart from them. Several unlit tables, without cutlery, a solitary young waiter hovering in the background, watching them.

Fred ordered a bottle of wine and they lingered over the dregs afterwards, toying with a few breadcrumbs lying on the tablecloth, watching the candle sinking lower, a dancing flame in a pool of molten wax. What they had spoken of, Edith could not have said with any precision, but it did not seem to matter. She felt contently tired now, with so much food, with drinking. She only knew she was with friends.

With the waiter hovering, showing signs of impatience, Fred settled the bill and they left, bundled up against the cold, thick gloves, scarves round their ears. They walked briskly under a high black sky, frosty with unknown stars, and saw the breath from their mouths forming a misty column. The streets seemed deserted tonight.

The house, when they got to it, loomed high, dark and forbidding. No light to be seen anywhere, even higher up, where the windows had not been boarded over. An eerie stillness, chilling their mood. Knowing the lights were not working in the stairwell, they cautiously made their way up to the first floor, but Martha could not switch on the light within their door either. Edith stood in their dark hall whilst Martha and Fred crept from room to room, trying the lights, which did not work. The dark rooms felt icy cold.

Must be a power cut.

But through the windows they saw lights burning in neighbouring buildings.

Whilst Fred got up on a stepladder to check their fusebox, Edith went up to the second floor. Her flat was also dark, and cold, with nothing functioning.

The three went down to the ground floor, and Fred flashed his torch round the cupboard under the stairs. Here were the meters, half a dozen of them, massive black boxes, ancient cables, heavy iron switches.

Must be the main fuse, but which is it?

It's too dangerous to touch.

I think somebody has been tampering with it.

You can't be sure.

No.

Edith had said nothing so far. Now she put in: I think we should try to ring emergency.

But the telephone was not working either, neither hers nor theirs.

Martha found candles, Fred brought out several paraffin heaters, and got them ready. He kindly took one up to the second floor, put it in Edith's bedroom, lit it for her. It was as though he had been living through a war, always, and knew just what to do now. Edith said goodnight to him, got into bed fully clothed, blew out her candle, and was soon asleep, dozing off in the smelly, stuffy atmosphere.

. 22 .

The inquiry did not establish just how the fire started, and the court brought in a verdict of death by misadventure. Although arson was a possibility, conclusive evidence was lacking. Faulty wiring might have begun it and, once started, other factors would undoubtedly have made the situation worse. The bad condition of the building, the fact that tenants had left garbage on the staircase, that on the night in question tenants had been using candles and unsafe paraffin heaters, such things could easily outweigh any likelihood of foul play. A waiter in a local restaurant testified that victims had been drinking a few hours prior to the conflagration. Although traces of petrol were found on the ground floor, the squatter or vagrant apparently living there was not found in the ruins, and could not be traced elsewhere.